THE SCARECROW'S QUEEN

MONSTER'S DUET, BOOK 2

NAOMI LUCAS AND MEL BRAXTON

Copyright © 2023 by Naomi Lucas and Mel Braxton

All rights reserved. No part of this book may be reproduced or transmitted in any form without permission in writing from the author.

Any references to names, places, locales, and events are either a product of the authors' imagination or are used fictitiously. Any resemblance to actual persons, places, or events is purely coincidental.

Painted Cover Art by Zakuga

Discrete Cover Art by Artscandare

Chapter Headers by AtraLuna

Edited by LY

CONTENTS

DEDICATION

For the monster readers

THE SCARECROW'S QUEEN

ONCE, I WAS FEARED by all who gazed upon me. For the past centuries I have served, defending my crops in solitude, bearing my scythe as an omen.

But when the crops aren't seeded, I find myself standing over a field of dirt and weeds.

It is *her* fault.

The female who has inherited the farm. She might be the new queen of these lands, but in her wake, she brings only ruin.

So I will scare her away. I will claim these fields, and she will learn to fear me!

Until one evening, she is attacked by the crows. She cowers behind me for protection.

Her terror and desperation stir me into action...

Nobody, not even a god, is allowed to frighten what is MINE.

PROLOGUE

HOLLOWSTALK

It was like any other winter day on Sylvie's farm. The cornfields were sheared low, jagged gold-brown needles sticking out from the dusting of snow, tight in their linear rows. Acres of dead crops surrounded me. They spanned out, opposing the horizon of a frozen morning sky interspersed with streaky white clouds. Clouds that would vanish by high noon, leaving nothing between the sun and me.

The farmhouse and barns sat undisturbed, the bordering forest still as stone. The road leading to and from this land was packed tight with cold dirt.

It was nearing midmorning, and old lady Sylvie had yet to make an apperance—which was unlike her. She rarely missed her tea and biscuits, let alone her searing perusal of the land from the front porch, always wrapped in her faded flannel robe. Through the dingy windows of her kitchen, nothing stirred. The drapes to her upstairs bedroom were closed, and there was an absence of smoke from the chimney.

Instead, crows gathered.

At first it was one or two at a time, pairs hopping around the dead stalks. They gave me a wide berth, acknowledging our pact. Except as the morning came to an end, their numbers grew to dozens. They gathered on the rickety wooden fence lining the road, the railing of the porch, the roof, and fields on either side, closing in on me. They settled on the branches of the forest. With each passing minute, more arrived.

During the cold months, we had a truce, they and I. There was nothing to destroy, no crops to eat, and so, there was nothing for me to protect. I did not need to scare them away, to ensure the harvest wasn't ravaged.

They weren't here for a meal. They would not disobey the Crow King today.

Their sharp gazes lingered on the house, and as more of them arrived, so did mine.

That evening, nothing changed. The farmhouse remained dark as the crows grew in their number.

And the next day, it was the same.

The same can be said for the next one too.

By the fourth evening, thousands of crows had gathered, so great a number they called forth their god. Large and menacing, his shadow wandered the farmhouse's periphery, silent and predatory. All through that night, he stalked the grounds.

The next morning he and the crows were gone.

A car arrived driven by a man I recognized, one who visited on occasion, both human and timeless. He let himself into the house, and shortly after, more vehicles appeared. They lined the dirt driveway, and their drivers met with the timeless man. They followed him into the house, and when they came back out, it was with a bulky bag on a gurney.

It was then, to my dismay, I realized Sylvie Shorewood, my queen, was dead.

CHAPTER ONE

THE INHERITANCE

DELILAH

Hissing between gritted teeth, I hit another pothole. To my dismay, the crumbling dirt road is littered with them. Each one ignites my nerves a little more.

The road goes on and on, winding through miles of farmland and forest, each territory sparser and larger than the last, still covered in late-winter snow. The few houses I pass are old and in need of repair, which doesn't bode well.

I'm never going to be able to sell my aunt's place if it's anything like these.

I'm going to be stuck with her land for the rest of my life, bleeding out property tax. The car dips, rattling over another divot in the road, and I tighten my grip on the wheel.

Aunt Sylvie left me everything in her passing, and I only have a hazy guess as to why.

She and my mom were estranged. Coming from a family with four siblings, all daughters, Sylvie was the eldest and my mother was the youngest. When Sylvie was in high school, my mother was in diapers, toddling around and eating Cheerios off the floor.

In her senior year of high school, she met and fell in love with a man named Ivar. They eloped that summer and moved to the upper Midwest to care for his family farm—the farm I've now inherited. My grandparents have never gotten over it.

And because of this, I've only met my aunt a handful of times.

Nobody in my family liked Sylvie. She had a penchant for the occult, the strange happenings of the world, and all things supernatural. She was likened to a witch, which bothered my mother—a woman who married a lawyer, moved into the hills, and preferred getting her nails done over dirtying her hands.

So, as my mother's only daughter, and the only grand-daughter in the entire family, Sylvie took a liking to me on her few visits west. She said I was special, the first and only girl born to my family's generation. She hoped to have a daughter of her own, one just like me. My aunt doted on me, told me all sorts of fantastical stories, and would sometimes send me gifts on my birthday. There was always another dream catcher, glass pendant, or fairy figurine.

Mom hated it. She didn't want my head filled with "rubbish."

The dirt road winds, and a white house, several barns, and a windmill appear. My inheritance is called "Crow's Rest," and the land seems to go on forever, the fields spanning far into the distance.

As I drive toward the house, I realize there's no gate barring the driveway. The only fence lines the driveway and is far more aesthetic than functional.

It's completely open. Anyone who wanted to enter could. As a little girl, I grew up behind gates and security cameras, and this new lack of security heightens my nerves.

My apprehension builds as I eye the forest across the road. It's thick and overgrown and could inhabit any number of wild animals.

Slowing down, I turn onto the gravel driveway passing endless rows of cut cornstalks on either side. Closer to the house, the front fields end in a large yard. On my left is a red barn with places to park in front of it, and on my right is a garden, a shed, and a gate that leads into the fields. There's a newer larger barn at the back of the house and an old windmill to the left of it.

Parking out front, I exit the car and stretch. Cracking my back, I take in the two-story white farmhouse with a wrap-around porch.

It's dingy with flaking white paint. The windows are dusty, and the columns along the porch are thin. Shaggy, overgrown bushes of all shapes and sizes—still dead from winter—line it in a messy array. Old planters hang from the ceiling containing withered shrubs. Mismatched tables and chairs are clustered throughout, and I spot a couple of colored glass ashtrays. The garden beds are crowded with dead plants.

A wind chime rings when a breeze blows by. Dry herbs secured by strings swing from where they hang along the walls and within the windows. Most of them are covered in spider-webs.

This porch practically has Aunt Sylvie written all over it.

I appraise it all, holding onto a shred of hope that someone will see past the house's rough exterior and buy it anyhow.

Checking the time on my watch, I have ten minutes until the executor of my aunt's will arrives with the keys. Hopkins is his name. He discovered her body.

She died in her sleep, in her bed with a book in her hand, from an aneurysm. There was no pain.

She simply... died. One minute here, the next, gone.

It wasn't until after she was buried that my family was even told. No one knew until my aunt's will was read—which speaks to how cut off she was.

I climb the porch and peek through the front windows. There's so much stuff. I can't believe it's all my responsibility. I live in a third-floor studio apartment in San Jose near the university where I studied kinesiology. I had no reason to move after landing a job at the fancy athletic club several blocks away.

Turning back, I spy a man standing in the fields.

Stiffening, it takes me longer than it should to realize it's a scarecrow and not some murderous lunatic. I don't know why I head straight for it, but one foot follows the next.

The scarecrow hangs on a long pole, flanking the right-hand side of the house and facing the property. Tall and standing on a rectangular wooden platform within the rows of cut stalks, he must rise above the crops even at full growth. There's a wooden stepping stool nearby, half-packed into the frozen dirt.

I shove my hands into my jacket pockets and look up.

Someone created him with care, and they made him well enough to trick me into thinking he was human for a split second. Cloaked in a faded black trench coat that hides much of the scarecrow's form, he wears matching black pants, a pair of muddy boots, and a bucket hat. There's a scythe crossed at his back, and a leather thong hangs from his neck. Something white dangles off it.

I pull the stool out of the dirt and use it to step onto the platform. Even here, the scarecrow is taller than me, and I have to reach up to identify what's on his necklace. I flip the white thing over.

It's a bird's skull. The thong is strung right through its eye sockets.

Cringing, I wipe my hand on my pants.

Patchy and coarse, his mouth is sewn into a grin, and for his eyes, there are two yellow beads stitched upon a black cloth. There's a slight bulge in the middle, indicating a nose.

Stringy black hair falls around the doll's face, sticking out from his bucket hat. Tufts of hay protrude everywhere, including the trench coat. Some of the sewing along his chest has come undone, revealing straw. He's stuffed with it, his arms and legs bulging under his clothes.

His hands are long, jagged sticks popping out from the cuffs of the coat, hanging from elbows that are propped up on either side of his body.

So creepy. What the hell, Aunt Sylvie?

Something hums behind me, and I turn to see a car down the road. It turns into my aunt's driveway.

Hopkins.

He parks next to my car. Our eyes lock, and he gives me a crinkly smile that reaches to his bushy brows. Slicked-back gray hair frames his wizened face, tied loosely at the back of his neck. He retrieves a cane and an envelope from the front seat as I reach him.

"Hopkins, I assume? I'm Delilah Mackey."

He straightens. "The niece."

"The one and only."

He leans on the emerald-studded cane as he studies me with squinty eyes.

"I think she mentioned a niece once, long ago. I'm sorry for your loss and for not contacting you sooner. No one considered Sylvie might have family elsewhere. She was a particularly private woman."

"It's fine. It's been years since I last saw her."

Hopkins smiles again as he looks around. "I wish I had visited more. I always liked this farm. Come—" he turns and waves me along "—and we'll talk inside where we can warm up and sit down. I'm sure you have a lot of questions." Drawing a ring of keys from his pocket, he heads for the front door.

A breeze swipes my hair across my face as something flies overhead. A crow swoops down to land on top of the garden shed. It caws and looks at me.

I brush back my hair and glimpse the scarecrow in the field behind it. Together they glare at me like they know something I don't.

"You coming?" Hopkins calls out.

Plastering on a tight smile, I head to the door. "I suppose it's called Crow's Rest for good reason?"

"The birds love that forest across the way, always have." He lets me into the house and hands me the keyring. "The keys have tabs on them for where they go. The house, the truck, the barns, the shed, you get it."

I file through them. "That scarecrow out front, did my aunt make him?"

"Ah, so you've noticed Hollowstalk. He's been out there for as long as I can remember. Him and that crooked grin of his."

I peer up at him. "He has a name?"

"Sure does. Something that ostentatious has to have a name."

"I guess I'm not the only one who's creeped out by him."

"That's his job, keeping the crows away and scaring off the occasional solicitor. Your aunt always liked him for that reason. Every spring she'd go out there, change his clothes, and fix him up. But she wasn't the one who made him. As far as I know, he's been around for as long as this farm. He was here when Ivar and Sylvie were newlyweds."

That's odd. I hesitate at the threshold.

"Ready to get down to business, Miss Mackey?"

I look over my shoulder and glance at the scarecrow once more before shutting the door.

I'm not prone to paranoia, but I'm getting rid of the scarecrow.

Following Hopkins into the house, I join him at the dining room table. I pull out my notebook and pen and flip to a blank page.

"Let's begin."

CHAPTER TWO
LAY OF THE LAND

DELILAH

I peruse the keys, flipping through them one by one and reading the faded labels. They're the only piece of my aunt I took with me back to San Jose as I set my affairs in order.

Besides taking unpaid time off from work, I sublet my apartment and packed all of my belongings in a storage unit until fall.

What I had blindly hoped would be a quick winter trip will now set my life back by months.

The farm isn't sellable without renovations, at least not at market price. The bank won't take it unless I cut a hundred grand off the top. Renovations would cost half of that. So, if I want my money's worth out of the place, I need to put in some work. That was what the realtor told me.

That was two months ago. Now, in the midst of spring, I'm here, ready to get to work.

My reward for all this effort? Enough cash to cover a down payment on a home of my own.

Aunt Sylvie left me enough money to fund the renovations. Luckily, according to the inspector, the house's issues are mostly cosmetic. If I can clear it out and make it suitable, I should make back the hundred grand and a good chunk more. A little elbow grease is all I need.

Sighing, I set the keychain on the nightstand, turn off the bedside light, and curl up under the stiff blankets of the airport hotel in Honey Falls.

Glimpsing several messages on my phone, I sigh again, annoyed that my parents won't leave me alone. They don't like any of this, and if I have to hear it one more time I might scream. I'm not exactly a fan of putting my life on hold either.

I'd rather be in San Jose than the upper Midwest. Yet here I am. I'm not going to give up on a hundred thousand dollars so easily.

But there's more to this than a down payment.

Aunt Sylvie left me everything. Her entire world. And I may never know why. Her belongings should be put to rest. I'm the only one who cares. My uncle Ivar died fifteen years ago, and she never had any children of her own. It'll be a sacrifice on my part, but I have the time and the resources to pull this off. I can make her home beautiful once more.

The next morning, I drive my aunt's truck along the long dirt road, surprised by how different my surroundings are.

The trees have bloomed, green with leaves, the fields lush and sprawling. Wildflowers line the quiet road, the ditch unplagued by litter. One farm has acres of gooseberry bushes beginning to flourish while another is topped with freshly aerated soil. When I roll down the window and take a deep breath, fresh air fills my lungs. The houses seem cleaner, their windows reflecting the sunlight. Gone is the snow-laden barren landscape.

In this new light, Aunt Sylvie's place is lovely, if unkempt. The cornfields have just a touch of green popping out of the ground.

Hopkins told me Sylvie's crops were her main source of income—soybeans, wheat, alfalfa, and *corn*. The best corn. It would regularly win in the state fair, so that's what she focused on. She was proud of its bright, bursting flavor.

Corn.

I know absolutely nothing about farming or growing corn—or any other plant or flower for that matter. I have one houseplant, and it's fake.

Stress churns my stomach as I scan the fields. Figuring out what to do with the crops is only one task on a long list of priorities, though Hopkins said there were local farmers I could contact for help or that I could hire a seasonal worker.

Parking in front of the house, I grab my suitcase and let myself inside.

The interior is as I remember it despite being dustier. Nothing has moved, nothing has changed. It's humid and dark, and there's a distinct smell of musty paper and potpourri. Faded pictures of Sylvie and her husband line the front hallway and along the stairs to the second floor. Directly to my left is the dining room, and behind it is the kitchen, pantry, washer closet, and a stairway to a dingy cellar. On my right is a sitting room that leads into a back den. The hallway ends with the downstairs bathroom, another entryway to the kitchen, and a backdoor that opens into a sunroom filled with dead houseplants.

Every room is crowded, each surface covered and cluttered. Books, crafts, and trinkets. All the same, Sylvie was tasteful amidst the hoard.

There are three bedrooms upstairs, including the master suite. The third bathroom is a Jack-and-Jill, connecting the two smaller bedrooms. The rooms are filled with everything from clothes and antiques to filing boxes with labels like *Taxes 1980-85*.

I make the small front room mine because the bed is the easiest to clean off. Once I'm marginally settled into the clustered space, I get to work.

Opening the windows, I gather all the cleaning supplies I can find and make a list. The house is my first priority. Once the inside is cleaned out, I'll begin repairs, some of which I hope to do myself, including painting, landscaping, and fixing the fence.

I'll need contractors for the electrical and plumbing. Both the furnace and water heater are outdated. And there's no central air—my aunt's room is the only one with a window unit installed.

There's also no internet.

Writing everything down helps me feel a little more confident, and I tear the list from my notebook, head down to the kitchen, and pin it on the refrigerator.

My phone rings, and my brother's name appears on the screen. "Hello."

"Mom and Dad are pissed." There's no greeting, no *how are you*. "You should've just taken the bank's money and called it a day! I just spent over an hour on the phone with Mom crying at me to bring you home! She's convinced you'll listen to me. I told her I tried but you're going to be an idiot anyway."

"Sorry you had to go through that," I say with sarcasm. "Sounds awful. If that's all, I have work to do."

"Come home. Now. Before Mom starts paying attention to me again."

Pacing downstairs, I open the drawers and cupboards, riffling through the contents. "I don't have time for this, Daniel. Next time just tell Mom to call me and leave you out of it. Otherwise, I'll see you this fall. Bye."

"Delilah, wait—"

I hang up and turn my phone on silent. Sometimes I hate being the baby girl, the *only* girl in the entire family. Massaging my temples, I look out the window. My eyes narrow on the scarecrow. My throat tightens as my fingers slow.

He's as creepy and unnerving as he was several months ago.

Dolls have never spooked me, but there is something about the scarecrow I can't quite place. Perhaps it's because his features are almost human and distinctly not. Maybe it's the way his glassy eyes glint in the sunlight, or perhaps it's because he *does* have a history. If what Hopkins said was true, Hollowstalk has been around longer than I've been alive.

To him, I'm the interloper, someone prepared to destabilize everything he has ever known.

The sooner I get rid of him, the better.

CHAPTER THREE

GOODBYE CREEP

DELILAH

Several weeks pass in a haze of activity.

Every day my mark on the house grows. I've cleaned out the front room and moved the single air unit out of my aunt's room and into mine, effectively making it the new master bedroom.

I might have died from heat stroke if I hadn't. I've tuned the old tube TV in the corner of the den to the local news station, and Weatherman Pete says there's an unprecedented heatwave and it's breaking records.

I'm a Bay Area girl, not a Central Valley lass, and the relentless heat wears me down like nothing else.

Since my arrival, I've trimmed the bushes, cleared the garden beds, and started composting the debris. I've cleaned out the kitchen and the sunroom and made progress on the piles of old paperwork littering the office. The bathrooms have been cleaned—and thank god they're better than I expected, especially the oversized claw-foot tub in the Jack-and-Jill attached to my room.

Gone are Sylvie's clothes and the entire rack of rusty paint cans in the shed. Gone are the dozens of vintage rugs that haven't been aired out in over a decade. I've sorted the canned food in the cellar, finding most of it to be good for another six months. The same is true for the hundreds of linens with moth holes and stains. Gone are all the broken appliances.

I had to rent a large dumpster for all the trash.

Two local antique shop owners are coming soon to review my aunt's tchotchkes and furniture. With the house cleared, I'll tear down the wallpaper that lines every room and paint. I'm debating warm whites and yellows and am already testing some swatches in anticipation.

It feels strange, clearing out my aunt's stuff and looking at her photographs on the wall all day. I feel like I'm in a stranger's house the more I learn. She liked western romances and Edgar Allen Poe. My uncle preferred history and war. She liked to preserve foods and collected costume jewelry.

She has an entire chest filled with Mardi Gras masks that I don't know what to do with because I secretly want to keep them.

There's also a case of recently cleaned rifles in the basement.

The biggest setback I've had is with the internet. Without improvements from the provider, it looks like I'm stuck with crippling speeds.

Yawning, I pour another cup of coffee. I haven't exactly been sleeping well.

Today I'm walking the borders and learning what's waiting for me at the edge of the property. Heat be damned.

Tugging on my boots, slathering on sunscreen, and donning a wide-brimmed hat, I grab my water bottle and head out the front door.

Too soon sweat beads on my brow and my lungs fill with hot, humid air. Cursing, I walk to the gate, determined to see how the fields are doing. Aunt Sylvie's records say she has an irrigation system installed, and the way the soil has gone from dark and rich to a dusty, barren brown suggests I should do something about it, and soon.

I'll never sell the place if everything is dead.

Huffing, I wipe the back of my hand across my brow and take a swig of water.

As I do, my gaze lands on Hollowstalk.

A dozen yards to my right, he's partially facing away but grinning at me all the same. The brim of his hat casts his face in shadow, darkening his hair and giving him a menacing edge. I head toward him, sit down in his shadow, catch my breath, and change my plans.

I'll walk the borders tomorrow.

He looks toward my bedroom window. He's there every night and every morning, his gnarled form staring up at me, bothering me, and I vow his time is done. Only I always forget, drawn toward another task.

Well, today's the day. He's finally coming down.

With the scarecrow at my back and the farm sprawled out before me, I notice several crows perched on the roof of the house and barn. Two more peer at me from the fence along the driveway. As I take another sip of water, several more fly from the forest and land on the house's roof.

"You're not doing a very good job, Hollowstalk," I mutter, putting my water bottle down. "Aren't you supposed to keep the birds away?" I arch a brow and tip my head back to study him.

His coat has fallen open, and his crow skull necklace hangs in the air. Bleached white and bright, the adornment soaks up the sun's rays.

"No matter," I say, sliding my gaze to the rope tying him to the pole. "I think you'll like retirement. I know I will." I climb onto the platform and circle the post, searching for the best place to detach him.

The rope is hooked under his elbows, and the majority of the knots are around the handle of the scythe crossed at his back. Securing my switchblade, I saw through the knots at the bottom and work my way up. One by one, the threads snap.

Behind me, the crows chatter. Glancing over my shoulder, I see some of them are watching me.

Hollowstalk sags as I remove the scythe from his back. Once the weapon is free, I toss it to the ground, eliciting a chorus of caws.

I swear there are even more of them now. I retrieve the stool from the ground and place it on the platform, stepping on it to detach Hollowstalk's elbows. He goes limp as his left arm drops, now hanging only from his right. His hat flutters to the ground.

Switching to the scarecrow's other side, I hesitate, drawn by Hollowstalk's hair. Taking his locks between my fingers, I tug gently.

They're not attached by glue like I assumed. Instead, the ends thread through his rawhide scalp.

Like human hair...

I sift my fingers through the umbra threads, finding his hair thicker than expected. From the top of his forehead to the back of his ears—he has ears—all the way to the back of his neck, each hair is individually attached. I frown, wrapping his soft hair around my hands.

Someone spent a great deal of time on him.

Lifting his hair to see his eyes, my stomach coils as the glass beads glisten like real pupils.

I release his hair and wipe my palms.

When I cut through his last band, he drops like deadweight, filling the air with dust and hay. I jump down after him, wipe my sweaty hands again, and clutch him under the arms.

"Why are you so heavy?" I whine.

Needing every ounce of my determination to haul his weight in the scorching heat, I drag him to the dumpster.

By the time we arrive, I'm dripping with sweat, covered in dirt, and exhausted, gasping for breath. After taking a few minutes to breathe and wipe the sweat off of my face, I haul his body over and into the garbage. When I push his creepy hand over the edge, I lose sight of him behind the metal grate.

I smile. "Adios. Enjoy your new home."

Listening to the cawing crows, I pretend they're cheering me on as I retrieve the scythe from the field and lean it against the shed. Afterward, I take a long celebratory shower and get on with my day.

CHAPTER FOUR

TRESPASSER

HOLLOWSTALK

The sun beats upon me as anger knots my insides.

I spend the day plotting, and under the light of a bright moon, I make my move.

Willing my jointless body to life, crow bones, hay, and straw crack. They break and reform, strengthening me. However tenuous, the power that binds me here fuels my creation.

The reek of machine oil, mold, and plant musk fills my fabric long before I gain touch or taste. Even an unpleasant sensation is better than none at all, and I cherish the stench. For centuries, all I have done is watch.

She embarrasses me in front of the crows, stripping their fear of me by tossing me away.

If Sylvie truly gave Crow's Rest to this woman, then she has disappointed me. She knew better than to toss me aside.

Delilah. I scowl at the thought of the new queen's name.

Crawling out of the garbage, I retrieve my scythe and hat.

The fields have not been seeded, nor have they been aerated, watered, or maintained. Uneven rows of seeds have taken root, countless weeds amidst their numbers. If she had given this limited growth attention, they could've produced enough, but what has sprouted now wilts under the relentless sun.

She bewilders us all, and the crows gather in the forest, watching curiously. We all wonder—what is she up to?

If there is no harvest, there is nothing to offer them.

If there is no food, they will go hungry.

And then the Crow King would be displeased. His gifts are rare, and he does not give them lightly. Because of him, this land is unlike any other in Bloomsdark County. Blessed by a god's magic, the queen must give an offering, granting the crows a portion of the harvest in exchange. She is required to provide enough to keep them fed through winter.

She risks breaking the pact, a very bold move. And if she does break the pack, what will I become?

If she will not work the fields, I must find a way to ensure the harvest.

Dragging my body across the grass and dirt, my frustration builds. Climbing to my feet and finding purchase within my stiff boots, I haul my weapon up with me, leaning upon the staff as I firm my grip.

I face the house with narrowed eyes.

A dim light shines through the closer window of the second floor. The queen's bedroom, I presume, since these lights are the last to turn off each night. There is a machine placed on a ledge that hums riotously. Shifting my scythe, I thrust point-first at the object. It crashes inward, eliciting a sharp cry.

My grin sharpens.

I head for the front door and try the knob, finding it locked. At my sneer, it clicks open, obeying my whim, and I cross the threshold. There is no place on the farm that I cannot go.

As I step into the dim space, I sense a presence behind me. I peer over my shoulder and out the door, finding there are hundreds of crows gathered in the yard.

They want my back turned. Hissing with annoyance, I return to the porch, slamming the door shut behind me, and locking it closed. The birds scatter, fleeing back to the forest without a single caw between them.

I return to gaze up at the illuminated window and inch the pane open with my scythe. When I let go, it slams closed, and shortly, the queen's silhouette appears. Our eyes meet, and she recoils, her terrified reaction restoring my grin. She is as easy to scare as the crows, her fear just as satisfying.

I know just the trick that will frighten her further.

After gathering rope from the barn, I return to my platform and reattach myself to my pole. The following morning I glimpse her again. She appears in the window and looks across the field, staring at me for a long moment.

She rubs her face and turns away.

Shortly afterward, she leaves the house with a small knife in hand, dressed for the day. Her hair is pulled back into a ponytail, slick and wet. Bangs shadow her face, ashen despite her tanned skin. There are dark splotches under her eyes, traces of fear still evident within them.

She stomps across the field with such vehemence that my threads tighten in anticipation.

She stops in front of my platform and eyes the new bindings that hold my body upright.

"It's not possible," she whispers.

How naïve is she?

She climbs closer, her lips poised in a frown. Her fear is replaced with disbelief. I ache to scowl, to jerk forward and send her fleeing—but the strength of my limbs is gone, my willpower depleted.

She unsheathes her knife and slashes my bonds. "I don't know how you got back up here or who's bored enough to prank me—" her voice heightens into a shout as she looks around her "—but whoever they are, they're going to soon realize that it's going to take a lot more to send me packing."

For a second time, I drop at her feet. My frustration returns, hot and fervent, desperate to put her in her place. I have a purpose, and I will make her see that. She drags me to her truck, hauls me into the back—scythe, hat, and all—and starts her vehicle.

With my gaze fixed on the sky, we drive away from the only world I have ever known.

CHAPTER FIVE

THE MUSEUM

DELILAH

By some miracle, my hands are steady on the wheel. The radio station, one of the few that reaches the farm, plays a countdown of country hits, though it's somehow down to number six and I don't remember the last several.

He moved. He stared up at me from the yard. His eyes glowed, and his grin twisted into a scowl.

My face wrenches with the absurdity of it. The scarecrow is just that, a scarecrow. His eyes can't glow and his mouth can't twist. The image of it shakes me, and I try focusing on the road ahead, my thoughts narrowing on reentering civilization and the safety that comes with it.

I knew it would be dangerous being at the farm alone, but I had at least hoped my presence would stay under the radar. Now I'm not sure. Elmstitch is a small town, and people already recognize me at the few stores I frequent.

No one recognizes me in San Jose.

It was just a trick.

Some local asshole must have thought it would be fun to scare me because I live at the end of a long dirt road. They're the ones who shoved my air unit, moved the scarecrow, and tapped at my window. And in my paranoia, I imagined the front door slamming close, because it was locked tight. Nothing else makes sense.

Regardless, something is wrong with the scarecrow. Every time I'm around him, I'm intimidated. At first, it was easy to ignore by staying inside the house, but last night went too far.

It's just exhaustion.

My air unit broke when it fell, making me furious. When I woke, my sheets were damp with sweat after sleep haunted by lucid nightmares. The final straw was this morning when I found him attached to his pole.

I'm certain that I trashed him in the dumpster. It took over an hour to cut him down, drag him through the field, and across the front yard. I couldn't have imagined it.

It isn't just the scarecrow. The crows have been strange too.

I haven't spoken with Hopkins since the day he gave me the keys. That day, we talked about my aunt and the farm. He gave me advice and his phone number, leaving it at that. He didn't share any sinister stories or allude to anything odd. He didn't mention anyone who might be a problem. Now he isn't picking up his phone.

Turning onto Main Street, I search for a parking spot.

I've passed the museum while in town for supplies. I've been meaning to stop in and say hi but haven't gotten around to it.

I just hope he doesn't mind me dropping in on him with Hollowstalk in the bed of my truck, a problem I hope to load off on him—but this is what he does, right? Collect strange things? Things that move when they shouldn't. Things with twisted grins...

I find a spot out front. Unlike most of Main Street, the museum is a standalone structure with alleyways on both sides.

Without checking if the scarecrow made it, I head straight for the front door. There's a sign that says *Closed for Lunch.*

Taking a deep breath before I break out in a sweat, my gaze drifts down the street, landing on the cafe next door. There is a poster of a mouthwatering smoothie on the front window.

I'm heading toward it when out steps the biggest man I've ever seen.

With long black hair, sharp features, and an Iron Maiden T-shirt, he looks completely out of place in a town like Elmstitch. He's joined by a primly dressed blonde with glasses. They laugh like someone just made a joke, and I move out of their path.

"Sorry," the woman says. "We didn't mean to block the way."

"No worries. I'm just waiting for the museum to reopen."

Her eyes widen. "Give me a moment, and I can open it now. Are you interested in a tour?"

She hands her iced coffee to the man, pulls keys from her purse, and heads for the museum. I chase after her. She unlocks the front door as her boyfriend—at least he seems like her boyfriend—eyes me curiously.

Her key clicks, and she props the door open. "Sorry to keep you waiting. We don't usually get visitors on Tuesday mornings."

"Actually, I'm here to speak to Hopkins."

"Oh." She pauses. "He's out of town."

Of course he is when I need him. "How long will he be gone? I'd like to donate something to the museum."

"He's going to be out for weeks. I could give you his number if it can't wait?"

"I've already called him. He's not picking up."

She laughs and mutters, "Typical," as her gaze drifts back to her boyfriend.

He's standing beside the bed of my truck, staring at the scarecrow with a frown on his face.

The girl joins his side. "Is that..."

Hollowstalk seems deflated, smaller somehow. Suddenly I can't help a newfound twinge of guilt. Maybe I should take him back...

He's far too lifelike.

For my sanity, he has to go.

"His name is Hollowstalk," I say. "He belonged to my late aunt. I thought Hopkins might want him. I know he was friends with her and because Hollowstalk is relatively creepy, I thought he might be interested."

"Late aunt? You must be Delilah, old lady Sylvie's niece! I'm sorry for your loss."

"It's fine. I barely knew her."

She nods.

"You know my name but I don't know yours," I say.

"Summer." She nudges the man next to her. "And this is Zuriel."

"Hello." He bobs his head, his long hair draping over his eyes as he faces me. "Hollowstalk is his name, you say?"

"Yeah, why?"

"No reason."

My brow furrows.

Summer covers her heart with her hand. She's quiet for a moment, and the way she and Zuriel are looking at one another, I swear they're having some sort of silent conversation.

"What's wrong?" I ask.

Summer sighs. "I'm sorry. I think I might be getting sick. Unfortunately, you'll have to wait for Hopkins before you can drop him off."

I give the building's facade a longer sweeping look, taking in the way the signage seems faded with age and yet remains impeccable. I consider the couple again—the way her hand clutches her chest and how strongly out of his element he seems. They clearly know something I don't.

"All right..." I give them a polite smile. "Thank you for your help. It was nice meeting you, Summer."

She smiles tightly in response. "You too, Delilah. I'll let Hopkins know you stopped by."

They head inside, and I'm left alone on the sidewalk with Hollowstalk.

Damn it.

There is no way I'm taking him back to the farm. If I do, I won't be able to sleep tonight. I look up and down the street, finding that I'm alone.

My gaze settles on a dumpster in the alleyway next to the cafe.

Cringing at my desperation, I pull Hollowstalk out of my truck and haul him away.

Twenty minutes later, it's done. He's gone for good, and I'm driving to the hardware store to buy a new air unit. There's a smoothie in my hand and a smile on my face.

CHAPTER SIX

A MURDER OF CROWS

DELILAH

The world feels lighter, the devastating heat easing with an onslaught of puffy white clouds. Everything about life is fine at this moment—the wind in my hair, the sun on my skin, the clear scent of rural air, and the empty bed of my pickup truck.

Everything is fine.

I've made up my mind—last night I had heat exhaustion or sun poisoning. That's what happened. Tonight I'll keep my yard lights on and watch for intruders. I'll get some great sleep, and everything will be okay.

My hard-worn cheer wears thin when I get to the hardware store and the clerk tells me the entire town is sold out of air conditioners. Shy of driving up to Honey Falls, where securing a unit still isn't guaranteed, I'm out of luck until the next shipment. I make a quick stop for groceries and return to the farm.

My foot nudges the breaks when I pull into the driveway.

There are crows everywhere. The fence, the roofs, and the fields are covered. They caw and cry, darkening the sky as I drive the rest of the way to the house and park.

I stay in the truck and look around. I've heard about a scary movie like this, where a woman is attacked by evil birds.

I debate making a run for it or retreating. It's the sight of the melting bag of ice on the passenger seat that makes up my mind.

Grabbing everything I can, I slowly open the door.

When none of them attack, I unload and gingerly make my way to the porch. The crows caw and do nothing more. I set down my groceries and open the door, shuffling everything inside and shutting it before they change their mind.

First the scarecrow and now the crows. Feeling uneasy, I peer outside the window to watch them for a time. They continue to gather. My eyes drift to Hollowstalk's empty pole where the largest group is. They peck at the wood perch, the dirt, and anything their beaks can reach.

I don't know what to make of it.

Maybe getting rid of Hollowstalk wasn't my brightest idea.

I shake off the thought.

The crows are still there come nightfall. I try reading one of my aunt's cowboy romances on the downstairs couch but barely make it through a chapter when the crows begin to shriek.

They cry and chatter, screech, and cackle. I peek out the window to find them flexing their wings and raising their feathers. Seeing me, they shriek, and I cover my ears.

I check the other windows just in case something had set them off. Like a bear or a wolf.

Or a scarecrow.

Seeing nothing, I double check that everything is locked.

With a sigh, I return to my book, hoping the birds will go back to the forest soon.

When they're still out there hours later, I retreat to Aunt Sylvie's office to get some work done. I flip through a stack of yellowed newspaper clippings.

At the bottom of the pile is a page with a rough edge, like it was torn from a book, written in the cramped handwriting I've come to recognize as my aunt's. I scan it curiously.

1823, Winifred Merriweather and her family settle on the outskirts of a small town called Elmstitch after being excommunicated by the town's priest.

Known as the first queen and a witch, she established the pact to enrich the land, resulting in prosperity for her family. She dies in 1860 from pneumonia and is soon followed by her two sons and husband.

I shake the strange wordage off, likening it to slang or antiquated designations.

1860, Lydia Merriweather, the widow of Winifred's son, inherits the farm, its pact, and becomes the second queen. She remarries a year later in 1856 to Jacob Hull. She names the farm Crow's Rest. She and her husband remain owners until their deaths in 1884, bequeathing the farm to their false friend, Howard Comings.

1885, Howard Comings, the first owner of Elmstitch Bank, inherits the land with no intentions of honoring the pact. He and his wife vanish Halloween of 1886 after they sell the entirety of the harvest.

1886, Mary Comings inherits the farm. She agrees to assume ownership of the pact and, in doing so, becomes queen until her death in 1940.

1940, Crow's Rest is inherited by Susanna Shorewood, Mary Comings' adopted daughter. Susanna remains queen until 1988 when she dies of cancer. Her widower husband and son become joint pactholders.

1988, Ivar Shorewood marries Sylvie Shorewood. She becomes queen and overseer of its pact. After Ivar's death, Sylvie remains queen until—

I flip the page over and it's blank. Flipping back, I search for the rest of the sentence, but it's not scribbled anywhere. Instead, an article that had been under the page grabs my attention.

It's from the Elmstitch Press and written about Sylvie winning first place at the state fair in the corn competition. There's an accompanying picture of her proudly holding a trophy, taken in front of the house.

A blurry shadow looms over my aunt's shoulder that I recognize as Hollowstalk.

Chapter Seven

THE ASCENT

HOLLOWSTALK

It's cold, and my strength saps. I attempt to clench my fist. Again and again, I try. I try to no avail. By the time I hear the roar of the truck's engine, I know Delilah is leaving me behind. I must move again.

I cling to my frustration, urging the straw to stiffen. The effort drains me further, and my patches reform. Men breathe, don't they? Mimicking them, I expand my chest by sucking in air.

The threads of the first queen's power remain, constant like an inescapable undercurrent. I'm tied to the farm, and it must be cared for. I grasp onto this magic and weave it with my essence, binding them tight as I form the facade of a man.

Only I do not truly know what makes a man, and so I fuse straw, hay, and crow bones, guided more by intuition than ingenuity. I prop up my essence in a way even I don't quite understand and complete myself with smooth skin.

Lurching, I grab my hat and scythe. I climb over the dumpster's edge, and straightening, I stride down the moonlit alley. It's late, the town is quiet.

The farm beckons as I wander back alleyways and down dark roads. It is only out of sheer luck that I am not seen.

I'm drawn to a forest and find a creek. My pace quickens. Thick trees soon surround me—hoots from owls, the squeaks of bats, and the scurry of critters.

Delilah is a problem I must solve. Sylvie was either inattentive in choosing her successor or had failed to properly prepare her. Still, I can't hate her. Not completely. Her negligence gives me a reason to move, and strange as these circumstances might be, I'm excited.

I stretch out my fingers and, one by one, curl each to touch my thumbs. *Hands*—they're a pleasure, one too many take for granted. I sweep my scythe, and it cuts upon the air with a *swish*. I chuckle, cherishing the thrum in my throat.

Testing out the strength of my legs, I leap across the creek.

Glinting red catches my attention—the eyes of the Crow King's emissary—and I stop in my tracks.

I nod at him in greeting.

With a piercing caw, he dives into my path. Landing on a branch above me, he shakes out his feathers with a rustle, looks away, and then settles his gaze upon me again.

I climb up the slope to meet him, and he flies away once I reach the top. I pause, taking in the bounty before me.

Dying embers illuminate a man sleeping near a fire. A pickup is parked not that far away, the bed full of bags and boxes. My nose twitches with the scent of whiskey as my gaze lands on the half-empty bottle of liquor within his reach.

I am struck by inspiration. If Delilah will not grow the crops, then I will do it.

I quietly rummage through the campsite, finding a T-shirt, and jeans. I comb my hair with my fingers, tying it neatly at the back of my neck. For a final touch, I don my old bucket hat.

There's a name on the duffle at my feet, black ink against the gray fabric.

Jack.

Picking up my newfound belongings, I walk through the night without stopping again.

Chapter Eight
THE CONTRACT

DELILAH

I wipe my eyes. Sunlight streams through the shuttered windows, and I wait for the first caw, but it never comes.

I clamber onto the couch and peek out the window. The yard is clear and Hollowstalk's platform is empty.

I exhale.

Good.

All the same, the pressure behind my eyes builds as my hand kneads the tweak in my neck. My muscles are tight, and I'm damp with sweat. I go to the kitchen and make a pot of coffee. I haven't slept well the last few nights. And even when I do, my dreams have been unsettling.

I jump at a rap on the front door. I'm not expecting anyone today.

They tap again, louder this time. Scurrying back to the front window, I try to see who it is, but the porch obscures my view. There are no cars besides my truck out front.

A neighbor?

Tiptoeing to the door, I peer through the peephole. A man I've never seen before stands on the other side.

He's tall with long limbs, wearing a worn gray T-shirt and faded jeans. His dark brown hair is trapped in a bucket hat, tied back at the base of his neck. His rugged appearance suggests he does physical labor for a living, and the same can be said about his sun-bleached clothes.

"What do you want?" I call out.

"I'm here for work," he shouts, his voice muffled by the door.

Maybe he's one of the laborers Hopkins mentioned.

Unlocking the door, I crack it open.

His expression is so sharp and discerning it startles me. I shake off the déjà vu, standing taller. I peg him in his mid-thirties, older than me by at least a decade.

He looks down at me. "Aren't you the least bit ashamed of yourself?"

Affronted, my lips pinch. "Ashamed?"

He waves his arm toward the fields. "The fields are a mess. I've never seen them kept so poorly."

Who the hell is this guy? I avoid looking at the wilting sight, glowering at him instead. I don't need some asshole telling me this, especially so early in the morning. "Is this seriously how you ask for work? I'm not here to play farmer. I'm here to renovate and sell. It wasn't nice to meet you. Bye."

I start to shut the door, but he puts his hand over the latch. He cocks his head, coming off as surprised.

"What?" I prompt. "I have coffee to get back to." Between the scarecrow and the crows, I'm way too tired for bullshit.

His eyes glint with a soft golden amber. "Sell?"

"Yes, *sell*. Who sent you out here? Was it Hopkins?"

"No one sent me. I've worked here for many years. If you plan to sell—"

I open the door a little wider. "You've worked here before?"

His brows arch. "Yes."

I assess him again. "So you knew Sylvie."

"I did."

"So you also know she's dead."

His lips twitch. "I heard gossip."

"You two weren't close?" I ask.

"Not particularly."

"What kind of work did you do for her?"

His face scrunches like my question is annoying, which in turn further annoys me. Except curiosity wins out, and I stall before shutting the door on his hand.

"I helped her with the fields," he answers.

The fields. The one part of this project I have no idea what to do about. Eyeing him again, I'm a little less annoyed.

"Okay. I'll hear you out..." I open the door wide. "So you know how to grow crops?"

"Of course I know how to grow crops."

"I haven't planted anything. I wasn't planning to—"

He rolls his eyes. "The sprouts that have wilted are beyond repair, but there is still time to sow. You could salvage a harvest, limited though it may be. However, the seeds must be planted immediately."

"And why would I want to do that?"

His nostrils flare.

Now *he* appears affronted.

"Why wouldn't you? Many seek the produce grown here. They rely on it, look forward to it, and are waiting for it. If there's no harvest, selling this place is the least of your problems."

"Are you saying there are... contracts?" My stomach drops. Among all my aunt's paperwork, I have yet to come across a single agreement about her crops.

"Yes," he says so nonchalantly my stomach plummets further.

He turns to the fields. My gaze drifts past him to the few crows that have reappeared amongst the scattered growth. They peck at it, tearing it apart.

"Great, the crows..." I say dryly then point to the birds. "Even if I manage to produce crops, there are so many birds. Last night, there had to have been hundreds gathered out here. They would ruin whatever comes out of the ground."

His eyes flick back my way. "They are curious creatures and not easy to scare away. You are right to be concerned. If left unchecked, they'll eat everything. Where's the scarecrow that used to be out front? Hollowstalk."

My lips flatten. "Why?"

Of course, he would know about Hollowstalk.

"It matters to me."

"I got rid of him."

His face pinches, then smooths out as a slight smile forms on his lips. "Well, that's your problem. He was the only thing keeping the crows at bay." He tsks. "I recommend you return him as soon as you can."

"I don't think that's possible. I dumped him in town."

"That's... too bad." He scowls at the birds. "I can handle your crows if you hire me."

"Hire you?" I cross my arms. "I can't afford much." Though it would be nice to have help with the fields. It would make it easier to sell.

"I don't need a lot."

I look around. "You don't have a car."

"I prefer to walk."

"You live close by? Because if you're looking for room and board..." I shake my head.

"Minimum wage is fine."

I eye him skeptically, alarmed that he suggested so little. Then again, he might not have a lot of options in a town as small as Elmstitch. "Sylvie's gone. Why do you want to work here? You could probably make more elsewhere. There are farms all over the county."

"Because..." He scans me up and down. "This place is important, especially to us locals. It's in both of our interests that this place sells to someone who will manage it better."

I should be affronted again, except he's not wrong. Someone else would value the fields more than me.

I can't believe I'm actually considering this. "Were you... and my aunt close?"

The surprise returns to his expression. "Sylvie was your.... aunt?"

"Why do you seem shocked by that?"

He mutters something.

"What?" I lean in.

He faces me with frustration brazen in his eyes. And I don't know why me being Sylvie's niece matters. "If it were possible, I would buy this land from you myself. Because if she chose you to take over and did not forewarn you to the hardship owning this farm can be, she failed you."

I frown. The more I talk with this guy, the more I dislike him. He eyes me, his features smoothing out once more. "Give me half of the harvest, and I'll help you maintain the fields until you sell."

I'm about to answer no when my lips snap closed.

It's a good offer. We both win. He wants the land to be cared for and can profit from the crops. And having tended fields will help it sell.

It's only one season. We won't need to put up with one another for long.

"Instead of minimum wage?" I ask.

"Yes."

"Works for me," I agree. If he wants the crops, I have no complaints. "Half of whatever you manage to grow is yours." I offer him my hand to shake, and for the first time in days, I feel like things might not be as strange as they seem.

He closes his hand around mine and squeezes a touch too tight.

"What should I call you?" I ask, tugging out of his grip.

His eyes glisten. "Jack. Jack Hollow."

"You start tomorrow, *Jack Hollow*."

CHAPTER NINE

THE UNWANTED HELP

HOLLOWSTALK

Running the farm is easier than I thought.

Delilah keeps her distance. It is clear she does not like my presence, and I prefer it that way. It is not easy to keep up my ruse even without being watched.

She's completely enthralled with fixing the house. I see her through the windows, and while she may not supervise me, I study her. If I am pretending to be human, I must learn to act like one.

It is for the best that she works on the house and stays away from the fields. She would only get in my way. My methods would confuse her, and if she saw, she would want an explanation.

The first week passed quickly and scattering the crows has become trivial. Since I became Jack, I have continued to keep them away. I carry my scythe as I work, reminding them of who I am despite my appearance.

I have even woven small charms, gathering ragweed into bouquets that now hang along the fence. These ensure the birds keep their distance when I am forced to rest. Like me, they're worried about this new queen, and I fear nothing will stop their approach if the second seeding does not sprout.

Planting anew has consumed my strength. This body tires in new ways, and to recover, I must often return to my platform where I can recover while hiding beneath the boards.

Stomping the earth, I frighten the pests. With the touch of my finger, the weeds shrivel. My breath encourages seeds to germinate. In my wake, the fields begin to recover. The land knows me, responding to the gifts Winifred gave me for its care.

It is a blessing to be alive in such a way. Being able to move is so... *liberating*.

My senses spark, and I catch sight of Delilah leaving the house with a trash bag. Glancing at me, she quickly tosses it in the dumpster and disappears into the barn.

As much as I enjoy her unease, frightening her no longer makes sense. As much as I loathe to admit it, I need her. At least until there is someone else to take her place.

Turning to the task at hand, I survey the nearby plants. The undeveloped raspberries are yellow and small, but they're growing fast despite their neglect. With all the other early produce growing poorly, they will have to be enough for a midsummer peace offering.

Walking to a leaf, I narrow my gaze on several aphid larvae. At my whim, they dry up and die, and I press their remains into the dirt so the dirt may gain their sustenance.

I'm about to do it again when I'm interrupted by a shrill humming noise and several knocks in quick succession. Standing, I glance at the house, searching for the source.

It's Delilah. Of course it's her. She's working beside the fence along the driveway, now carrying a large board that's way too big for her. She wobbles as she drops it, and I hasten to her side.

"What are you doing?" I growl.

She pushes her hair out of her face and looks up at me warily. "The boards are rotted through." She points toward the fallen section of fence where one of my ragweed bouquets is crushed upon the ground. "I'm taking them down so I can replace them with new ones."

Scowling, I lift the plank, retrieve the ruined charm, and wave down the fence line. "Are you planning to take them all down?"

"The rotted wood needs to go. A new fence will help the curb appeal of the house, one that's not covered in rot, bird crap, and rust."

"How is a fence more important than the crops?"

Her face flushes.

"You do your work and I'll do mine." She wrinkles her nose as her gaze casts down the field. "Not that I understand what you're doing out here all day. You barely touch the equipment. You use the irrigation system and walk around the farm. You make these... *trinkets*." She nods at the bouquet in my hand.

I am mistaken. She has noticed me.

Arching a brow, I point to the fields. "The crows are gone, and the seeds are planted. The ragweed repels the crows."

She mutters something that I can't hear.

For a long moment, we glower.

Then she sighs. "I'm replacing the fence. And to do that, I need to clear these things, these plants..."

"Charms."

"These charms are in the way. So, tell me, how can I do this without disturbing them?"

"I'll take them down. I'll attach them to the new fence."

"Thank you."

I nod.

"For what it's worth, I'm only planning to replace the first four sections today," she adds.

Sauntering past her, I collect the ragweed. The crows chatter—*laughing* at me, and my body clenches. I bare my teeth, and proving I am not to be trifled with, I tap the pole of my scythe against the ground. They hush.

When I am done, I turn to face Delilah, finding her staring at me like I'm crazy. All the same, she says nothing as I stride past her. I feel the weight of her eyes following me as I walk away.

Chapter Ten
A Windmill in Decline

"Jack!"

Far off, Delilah shouts my name.

I lift my head, surprised she's calling for me. We don't interact unless it's necessary. She has her tasks and I have mine, an arrangement which keeps us happily separated from one another.

She likes to argue with me, and I have no patience for it. With how little interest she has in this place, I'm amazed she's allowed me into the fields at all. Raising the crops would be much harder if I had to remain hidden.

She's different up close when I'm interacting with her like a human. She doesn't strike me as someone who would be irresponsible, and it's hard to understand why she is unbothered. If she produces nothing, a beautiful house won't save her from the Crow King's wrath.

He will not take failure well, especially if his minions suffer for it.

I will make certain that never happens, for my sake more than hers.

I look across the overgrown graveyard. At the edge of the land, at the back right corner of the field, lies a few small graves. Even without the cornstalks hiding them from view, the graveyard is easily lost in the surrounding forest, the low tombstones barely visible amongst the brush and overgrown weeds. The Shorewoods never maintained it, and so the wilds have reclaimed the small slice of land. It's become my favorite place to rest during the day.

Delilah doesn't wander this far. She rarely leaves the house and its grounds, and when she does, it's to go to town.

The house is so far off in the distance that its outbuildings are mere dots on the horizon. She could be looking in my direction, and I'd be too far for a human to see. I'm safe here, amongst the dead. I have privacy, a feeling I have come to enjoy. I can drop my performance without worrying about the watchful gaze of others—without *her* gaze.

Lowering my chin to my chest, I kneel before the first queen's tombstone, weathered and hidden in the grass, her name long since faded away.

It is nice to finally visit her grave.

"Jack!"

I scowl, hearing my name again. Faint as it may be, I'm certain it's coming from the old windmill.

Tightening my limbs, I stand, check my mouth for threads, and stretch. Listening for Delilah's voice, I wander toward the house. I take my time, watching the sky for trespassers and following the longer route, walking along the brook that lines the property and then meandering down the dirt paths trailing through the newly sprouted fields rather than cutting straight through.

The tallest building on the farm, the windmill was built at the back left corner of the yard and behind the old barn. Once, long ago, it was a prized possession but has since fallen to neglect. It's now used for storage.

Delilah shouts my name again. "Jack!"

There's a hitched edge to her voice that I didn't hear before. I pick up the pace, quickening into a jog across the yard. The windmill's doors come into view, one of them partially open. My ears prickle at the sound of a pained groan and a gasp. Growing alarmed, I take to a sprint.

"Ja—"

I rush into the windmill. "I'm here."

"Oh, thank god," Delilah gasps.

She's nowhere in sight, and I search in the direction of her voice, following it above me. She sits at a strange angle on the interior stairs, her right leg dangling through a broken step. One hand is balanced on the outer wall while the other clutches a wooden rail. Sweat sheens her brow.

"The stair broke. I was going slow, but I didn't realize the steps might be rotting. I can't climb out." She jerks as I head for the stairs. "Jack, don't!"

I shoot her a glare. "Why?"

"If the steps won't hold my weight, they definitely won't hold yours. They're coming apart. I can't move," her voice ends in a rush. "I tried. I'm stuck."

As she says this a piece of rotted wood falls from the step below.

She's right. She is stuck. I move under her and reach, brushing her shoe with my fingertips. "You shouldn't have gone up there."

"They only started cracking when I got here. I didn't know."

"What could you possibly need up there?" I reproach, looking around at the few old storage crates that could crumble as easily as the stairs. "I need a ladder."

"I wanted to see what condition everything was in before I hired an inspector to look at it."

I scoff and shake my head, eyeing the wood on either side of her. If it's cracking under her weight, I need to get her down now before her endurance wanes. Humans are weakened when they're hurt.

She'll be hurt if she falls.

She can't even climb stairs right.

I jog to the backyard barn where I last saw a ladder. When I return, Delilah watches in silence as I set it up, stretching its length until the top of it brushes her foot.

Climbing up to her, I notice a long scrape down the side of her calf. Tiny beads of blood spot her wound, her leg marred with dirt. *She did hurt herself.*

I imagine her scrape is painful.

My nostrils flare. I might not know what pain is, but I know it's something humans avoid—something they fear. And if I understand anything, it's fear.

"Shift your weight onto the ladder," I order.

"You think I'm an idiot, don't you?" Her voice is low, almost... sad, but she does as she's told.

"I think you need to check your priorities."

"We have different priorities."

To climb through, she needs more space, and so I grip the remaining part of the step, yanking it off. Screws and chipped wood pebble the floor.

"Jeez!" She peers at me through the gap. "Don't hurt yourself too."

"I won't. Can you put your other leg through?"

I climb as high as I can go, ready to catch her if she falls. Her left foot is perched precariously on the creaking step below.

"I think so."

She lifts her foot and slowly sets it on the ladder but immediately retreats, catching herself with a hitch.

"It's sprained," she whispers sharply. "Damn it." She dangles her foot above the step, favoring it, leaning on her hand that's still bracing the wall.

"Can you still climb through?"

"Yeah, I think so." She licks her lower lip. "Give me a minute."

I lick my lip in reaction, wondering why she does such a thing.

She shifts to her side and slips through the hole, sliding her hand down the wall as she goes. When she's crouched on the top of the ladder and starts to duck her head through, I gently cup her hip to guide her.

She looks down at me with a flash of something in her eyes before shuffling onto her butt and angling her legs my way. Whatever it was, it's gone by the time I catch her gaze again.

I lean back, remaining behind her, braced for any misstep as she turns and climbs the rest of the way down.

Finally safe on the ground, she sits on the ladder's third step with a huff. "Thank you." She bends her leg to inspect her scrape.

"Next time, don't climb old stairs."

Her face falls as she looks up at me. "I promise, I won't."

"Get me if you are ever worried about your safety. There are countless ways to get hurt around here. I don't want to see you in danger, weakening yourself unnecessarily." I wave at her leg. "You should do better at avoiding pain."

She looks at her wound and gives a small shrug. "You don't need to worry about me. I'll be far more careful going forward."

"Good."

"I really mean it, Jack. Thank you." She sighs and rubs her eyes. "As stupid as that sounds, for a moment there, I was afraid I would be stuck that way forever. I'm so glad you heard me."

"You're..." My words trail off.

I had taken my time responding to her and even ignored her at first.

Something I don't like cramps my chest. I eye her scrape, further stricken with unease. Perturbed by the sensation, I head toward the door before I show it. "Don't get hurt again."

She nods and stands, letting loose another sharp intake of breath that drops her back to her seat.

"I forgot about the sprain," she curses.

I close my eyes and reopen them, blanking my expression before turning back for her. Sighing, I clutch her arms and haul her to her feet before she can protest. Surprisingly, she leans into me, hovering her foot above the ground.

With her body pressed against me, she's soft and unassuming, slight compared to me. Her form fits, tucked inside my arm's embrace. She's warm like the sun.

Stiffening, she pulls away to hold on to my arm instead.

"That won't do." I tug her back toward me.

Her grip tightens. "What are you doing?"

I reach around her shoulder and pick her up, draping her legs over my other arm and cradling her against my chest. "Carrying you."

Taking her back to the house, I nudge the front door open and deposit her on one of the chairs in the front room.

Her gaze hooded, Delilah eyes me warily. "I would have managed."

I step away. "Crawling on all fours? Like a dog?"

She cringes. "No, not like a dog, like a girl whose pride is bruised."

"Is this pride worth further embarrassment?"

"Embarrassment? I'm hurt!"

Infuriating. I absently rub my chest. "Right, and I saved you the trip."

She brushes her hair back and lets out a short laugh, oblivious to how she annoys me. Curious by this sudden change, I search her face.

"Thank you," she repeats.

"What for this time?"

"For making me feel better and helping me inside. I want to apologize for..."

There is only one apology I care about. "Not seeding the farm?"

She laughs, waving the idea away. "No. I'm not sorry about that."

"Don't you fear the consequences?"

"Consequences?" She squints up at me. "Jack, I can't find any contracts. And besides, you seem to be doing a better job caring for the field than I ever could—"

Despite her alarming nonchalance, I straighten at her praise.

"I just wanted to say I'm sorry if I've been unwelcoming. You've helped so much already, and I'm glad you're here. I'm glad you arrived when you did. Things were getting... strange, but it's better now. It's been a huge relief." She smiles up at me.

She's happy?

"Good." I don't know what else to say, and I head for the door, giving her one last glance, wondering if this is what humans call a joke. To my continued surprise, her eyes are warm. "Shout for me if you need me. I'll keep an ear out for you."

"I—I will. That goes for you too."

Leaving the house behind, I return to the graveyard, confused. I've never made anything happy before. I was created to frighten, not to bring comfort or joy.

It's also becoming increasingly clear she knows nothing of her land, neither its history nor the responsibilities that come along with it. It doesn't make sense. Sylvie had never failed before, so how could she fail in preparing her heir?

My chest cramps anew, and I press my hand over it, searching for damage. There's no cut, nothing to justify the sensation, and yet, I discover my chest has become... *warm*.

CHAPTER ELEVEN

THE DILEMMA OF JACK HOLLOW

DELILAH

Hollow. I hate that his last name is Hollow. The worst part is I don't think Hollow actually is his last name and he's just saying it to keep me on edge. What are the odds his name would be similar to that of the scarecrow?

Then there's the scythe he carries when he walks around the fields. It reminds me of the scarecrow too.

I pick up my drill and get back to work. The bit whirrs, loosening the old screw, and I throw it in a bucket. Again and again, I do this until my arm is shaking and the power tool is hot. Hauling off one rotted board after another, I fill my wheelbarrow.

I've been working on this fence for days and am worn out.

I roll the barrow to the dumpster, passing Jack carrying that stupid scythe of his. I've decided not to question him about it because ever since I sprained my ankle, we've been on better terms.

I've seen him around more. Almost like he's keeping tabs on me. I can't help feeling like an idiot, like he can't trust me, or like I'm missing some sort of point. And whatever his point is, I don't care. I don't have time to care. I'll lose my job if I don't return by Thanksgiving so every day counts, and I can't imagine a harvest matters for anything more than appearances.

Not only that, but I've searched the house high and low and haven't come across a single document describing a contract. If there's no paperwork, how am I supposed to be liable for an agreement?

Even if he's frustrating, having him around has been useful.

I sit back on my heels with a huff, eyeing the yards of fence ahead of me. There's a lot more rotted wood than I anticipated. When I grip the next board, it snaps in half as I rip it free. Landing on my butt, I curse and toss the pieces aside. Lying back onto the grass with a sigh, I stare up at the cloudless sky.

After a few minutes, a *whoosh* fills my ears.

Curious, I straighten and look around.

One by one, sprinklers turn on across the fields, spraying the air with waves of misty hot water.

Wavering rainbows form within the water, and I rise to my feet, awed. Everywhere I turn there are more, lending the fields a magical guise. The scent of wet soil wafts past my nose as soft humidity rushes my face. Caught in a breeze, wayward droplets brush my cheeks.

Lips parting, I lift my face to the sky.

Lost in the moment, all my stress fades away. Refreshed and happy, I don't notice when Jack reappears, now shirtless and dripping wet, until he's striding through the corn rows and toward a dry patch of land.

He glances in my direction, and I quickly look away.

But I can't help taking another peek. When his back is turned to me, I gawk.

Rivulets of water cascade down his muscled skin, flowing along his toned edges and collecting along his waistband. He's not wearing boxers. I squint—he can't be. I'm debating whether to be grossed out or impressed by his choice when he turns slightly, causing the sunlight to glisten off his tapered pelvic bones which vanish into his jeans.

I squint harder.

Maybe Aunt Sylvie knew what she was about when she eloped with Ivar.

They don't make men like Jack on the coast. He's not like the weightlifters, wave catchers, and coders I'm often surrounded by. And though there's nothing wrong about those types of guys, Jack's got a body formed by labor.

Kneeling, he sets down his scythe and fiddles with something in the dirt. His biceps bunch, his focus rapt on whatever it is he's doing. His hair is plastered to his skin, coiling at his shoulders.

Jack is attractive and not in the classical sense. Something is unnerving about his appearance that makes watching him fascinating. He's distracting with an appeal that puzzles me.

The heat is doing something to my head.

He stands and wipes his gloved hands as water jets around him, spraying in wide arcs. With a pleased expression, he surveys his work, turning back in my direction.

Our eyes meet, and I stiffen, quickly glancing away again. My gaze lands on my truck, and suddenly I'm struck by a raging fantasy where I'm held down and bent over the hood as he thrusts into me.

Fuck.

I throw my gloves into my bucket, grab the drill, and head inside. In the kitchen, I splash cold water on my face and pour a glass of water, downing it in one go.

Fuck.

Wiping the water off my face, I groan and toss my washcloth into a nearby hamper. I've been reading way too many of Aunt Sylvie's romances. I should switch to Edgar Allan Poe.

Something moves in the corner of my eye.

Right outside the window, a large crow sits on the flower ledge beneath it. With red eyes, it watches me. I set my glass down, stunned—it's the biggest crow I have ever seen.

Almost three feet in length, his body fills the window.

My phone rings, sending my soul straight out of my body and into the heavens. Closing my eyes and clenching my fists, I count to five before pulling my phone from my pocket. When I look up, the window is empty.

I jerk forward and search the yard, checking the sky, finding the bird gone.

Drawing back, I lift my phone to my ear. "Hello?"

"Hi, Delilah, this is Hopkins. Summer said you were trying to reach me."

Oh. *Oh.* "Yes! Hopkins. Hi." I turn away from the window and lean my hip against the counter. "Sorry, I tried calling, but I couldn't get through."

"That's probably my fault. My job often takes me to places with signal worse than Elmstitch."

I chuckle. "Is that possible?"

"What did you need? Is your aunt's farm treating you well? I heard you might have something for me."

"I'm okay. It was Hollowstalk. I thought you might be interested in having him."

"So you've decided to get rid of him after all. Summer said you might."

"Well, actually, I already have. Sorry if that's not what you wanted to hear."

"Oh."

"Oh?"

"I would have taken him."

I hesitate before walking out to the front porch to check the platform. "You would have? Why?"

"Hollowstalk is one of a kind. He's as old as Elmstitch. He's even mentioned once or twice in the town's archives over at the library."

"I didn't know. I found him frightening."

Hopkins laughs. "Dear, he's supposed to be frightening."

There's a pause as I rub my brow, my chest constricting with guilt I'm annoyed at for feeling. "I'm sorry I didn't keep him for you. Thank you for calling me back."

"Of course. Goodbye, and good luck, Delilah. I hope you don't need it. Give me a call if you have any other frightening things you want to get rid of. Like me, Sylvie had a penchant for the bizarre."

He hangs up before I can say goodbye or ask him anything more. Putting my phone away, I search the front yard feeling like something is watching me.

When the only thing I see is a butterfly fluttering over the garden, I shake my head, berating my paranoia. I'm imagining things. That's all. I need a break.

Chapter Twelve
MIDSUMMER DAY

DELILAH

Securing the final board of the fence, I stand back and admire all I've done.

The wood has been replaced, and while I still need to stain and spray paint everything, I'm satisfied. The fence's straight and clean panels make the entire place more inviting.

Pleased, I smile and stretch.

Now today's work is done, there's plenty of time to rest before the Bloomsdark County Midsummer Festival, an Elm-stitch tradition where the locals gather to celebrate the longest day of summer. There will be fresh produce, food carts, live music, and slushies.

If anyone deserves ice covered in strawberry syrup, it's me.

Jack strides past me, placing his ragweed on this final stretch of fence. His steps are quick and efficient as always. Despite his long-limbed form, he's graceful, coming across as self-assured and confident. Two things I struggle with. I want his approval. It's a desire I can't shake, which is annoying.

"Are you going to the festival?" I ask.

He gives me a blank expression.

"The Midsummer Festival," I repeat. Surely he knows about it, being a local. There are advertisements everywhere. "I was told everyone goes."

He seems at a loss for words, which is odd. He always has plenty to say. "Everyone will be there? Will it be a good chance to meet other farmers?"

"Yeah..." I shrug. "I believe so... I think. The festival grounds are right down the road next to Cole's gooseberry patches."

His eyes narrow.

Unwittingly, I straighten.

"Are you going?" he asks.

"I can't resist the siren's call of strawberry ice and live music."

He nods gravely like he understands. "I do recall the festival. Sylvie would go there after she gave her gift."

"Gift?"

Jack's eyes shift away. "She fed the crows whatever was ripe. She did it to appease him, and it did."

"*Him?* I don't understand."

"Of course, you don't. She never told you any of this stuff, did she? How else do you think she grew the finest crops?"

It's been a month since anything overly spooky has happened, but I'm far from confident. There are random appearances from the giant red-eyed crow. And there are small hauntings that happen now and then—footsteps at night, swaying stalks as if someone was walking through them, and the feeling of being watched. My nightmares have returned. The last thing I need is Jack mentioning my aunt doing weird things with men.

"My aunt and I rarely spoke. I guess she must have had a lot of fun in her life." I try to lighten the mood while also changing the subject.

Jack doesn't respond, his gaze narrowing again.

Licking my lips, I struggle to hold his gaze. "You can come with me if you'd like. We can take the truck."

His lips flatten, and embarrassment coils within my stomach. "Not like a date, I mean—do what you want. You can have the time off either way."

For a moment, I'm afraid he'll call me the lazy, entitled heiress that I am. It doesn't matter that I left my parents after high school and have been financially independent since. My brothers can't say the same.

His attention moves to the fields. "Perhaps I will go. It sounds interesting."

A smile teases my lips. "So you'll come with me?"

"I haven't decided yet." Without saying more, he walks away, through the gate and into the stalks.

Cheeks burning, I pay no mind to the obvious rejection—did I seriously expect him to say yes?—and retreat to the house.

Today is going to be good no matter what.

Walking through the house, I search the windows for the large crow. Maybe I should call him Redeyes. He'll be less scary if he has a name.

By late afternoon, I hear the hum of the festival music down the road.

"Jack?" I call out curiously, stepping off the deck. When there's no answer, I take a couple of steps into the yard to peer around the house and check the back barn.

A row of baskets is neatly lined up along the garden bed. Curious, I walk closer, finding them filled to the brim with raspberries from the bushes.

Spying a few crows about, I open the garden shed and carry the baskets into it to deal with later.

When I'm done, I still don't see Jack anywhere, and I try not to let the twinge of disappointment bother me. Sighing, I pat down the skirt of my blue summer dress, and tuck it under my butt, saddling my bike. There's no point in driving the truck if it's just me. I pedal down the driveway and turn onto the road, searching one last time for Jack.

I settle into a leisurely cadence. Having the road all to myself, I relax and enjoy the fields and forest.

Country music strums through the air, the tune carried by a tenor voice. As I near the grounds, it's joined by the shouts of children, the hum of generators, and the smell of kettle corn. I lean my bike against a nearby fence and lock it. Fanning out my hair, I take off into the crowd. Sights, sounds, and smells overwhelm me. For months, the farm has consumed every waking moment, and I've forgotten there's life beyond the cornfields and constant repairs.

Surrounded by couples and families, I listen in on their conversations. The familiarity makes my chest ache for my own family, even if we fight often.

I head for the slushie stand.

Drink in hand, I shuffle to the side and gather my bearings. Music thrums from the stage, and all of the seating is already taken up by older couples resting their feet.

My gaze wanders to the vendors, narrowing on a booth where the Hopkins' Museum signage is displayed. Wandering closer, I recognize Summer standing behind a table where she addresses a small crowd.

"The beak of a giant Corvidae," she says, lifting it in her hand.

It's as large as my head. My throat is suddenly dry.

When I move closer, Summer sees me and smiles. "It's one of the few artifacts that's local. Shortly after the museum opened, it was donated by the hunter who found it. Several ornithologists have examined it since, determining it's real. However, nobody has found further evidence of crows this size—neither remnants nor sightings."

For a moment, everyone is silent, but then a teen at the front points to a jar of rusty nails labeled *From Sherry's Haunted Shed,* and Summer lowers the beak and starts in on another story.

Behind Summer, Zuriel and Hopkins speak quietly to one another. When Hopkins notices me he raises his cane in greeting. I debate telling him about the crow but admitting that I've seen a crow of this size would mean some of my delusions are real and can't be explained away by exhaustion.

The tension fades as I leave the booth behind. I wander through the stands until I see a woman selling salsa and, more importantly, grilled corn, the cobs skewered on sticks. Her food is locally sourced.

"You have corn from Crow's Rest?" I ask, confused that it's listed on the sign.

"From last year's harvest. I make the most delicious salsa from it." She points to a row of jars to her left. "Whatever I don't use, I freeze. It's not quite the same as having it fresh, but there's no time like midsummer to celebrate the fruits of last year's labor, and with the previous owner deceased, this might be the only corn from Crow's Rest we'll see this year. I had to unthaw it and bring it along."

"I'll have one."

"Good choice." She pulls a cob from the back of the grill toward the hotter front.

Middle-aged, her dark hair is interspersed with wisps of gray, framing a face worn by sun damage. Tiny in frame, she wears a yellow apron with frills along the edges.

"If you've never had Sylvie's corn, you can't rightly call yourself a local. Shame she's gone. We were two old lasses managing farms by ourselves and would often trade recipes. I'm going to miss her."

"I didn't know her very well. I wish I had."

The woman squints, searching my face. "Ah, I see the resemblance now! You're her niece. It's in the eyes."

"Delilah," I offer my hand, not entirely surprised she knows who I am. "I guess it's a small town."

She laughs. "Smaller than you think. I'm Miranda. I'm sorry you didn't know your aunt."

I wave away her apology. "It's nice to hear about her. I'm learning more about her as I go. Were you two close?"

"We ran in similar circles. But what about you, are you holding up okay? How is the farm treating you?"

"It's been good so far," I tell her. "But I'm only here long enough to take care of the estate. When the renovations are done, I'll sell and go back home."

Her brows arch. "You're planning to sell?"

"I have a job and a home in California."

"That's a real shame. If you change your mind, I think you might find you'd like it here."

I smile, touched by her sweetness. She removes the corn from the grill, drizzles butter over it, and hands the oily stick to me. "Enjoy the corn, Delilah. It's delicious."

I accept the cob. "It was nice to meet you."

"You too, dear."

Grabbing a few extra napkins, I meander back toward the stage. Finding a place by the fence, I lean against it and check out the corn.

I turn it over, and it doesn't look out of the ordinary. Maybe the kernels are plumper, though I'm hardly an expert. I take a nibble and they burst, flooding my mouth with sweet juice. I moan and take another bite. I finally understand the obsession with this vegetable.

Clearing the cob completely, I imagine what my mother would think if she saw me wiping butter off my chin.

I purchase a glass of Reisling to wash it down and return to my spot at the fence to enjoy the music. Dancing couples fill the space in front of the stage while others sway on the grass. I sip my drink and watch as fireflies appear.

Once again, I find myself searching for Jack, curious if he decided to come out tonight, wondering who he would show up with if he did. I never asked if he was seeing someone. I should have asked.

Scanning the crowd, I make eye contact with a blond man by the stage. For a moment, we watch each other. He waves.

I wave back.

He smiles.

I try to smile too, only my lips won't move. My mood fades, and I tip back the rest of my drink.

I catch sight of billowing thunderheads on the horizon. Seeing a large shape in the clouds, I squint, but it goes blurry before disappearing altogether.

Shaking it off, I head home.

Chapter Thirteen

A Pretty Flower

A festival would be a great place to find a new pactholder. With this thought, I wander the fields, debating if I should go.

I swipe my hand across the stalks as music swells in the distance. I haven't set foot off of the land since the night I returned.

Now I imagine leaving the farm of my own volition, on legs that I can only move because of Delilah's need for me, to seek out another who may take over, ensuring I will live for many harvests yet.

My chest burns with the thought. I am not one to be disloyal. Pulling off my hat, I thread my hand through my hair, drawing it out of my face. I scowl at the farmhouse.

Life was easier before Delilah when all I had to worry about were the crows. Sylvie's failure has been a nuisance.

The door to the house opens. Not wanting Delilah to see me, I duck out of sight around the corner.

She looks...

I lose the word as she walks off the porch, looks around, and then disappears around the house. She returns shortly, her eyes still searching. When her gaze streaks my way, I step into the barn.

With a disappointed expression, she smooths out her skirt and picks up her bike.

Her hair is down which is unusual. She always wears it tied back and away from her face. Now, it tumbles over her shoulders in long, soft waves, the tips brushing her lower back. My gaze trails over the rest of her.

The word I'd lost pops into my head.

Pretty.

Delilah looks pretty, like the flowers in the garden. I never understood the colorful, pointless plants. They would be snipped and brought inside to decorate the tables and windowsills but were otherwise useless. Sometimes people would stop, bend down, and smell them. Their eyes would close and a smile would appear on their lips.

I touch my mouth. There is no smile on my lips, and I'm too far away to bend down and sniff her.

She throws her leg over the bike and saddles it, bunching her skirt under her butt. Her expression shifts from disappointment to excitement as she pushes her foot down on the pedal. As she turns onto the road, I step away from the barn.

Debating whether or not to follow her, I'm already down the driveway by the time I decide.

Passing by forest and fields, I barely notice any of it, completely focused on catching up to her. All too soon, I lose her around a curve.

I keep following.

I see her next by a fence at the edge of a lot full of parked vehicles.

Hundreds of people are gathered just past them—more than I have ever seen in my life. Unusual scents flood my nose as I near. The music is louder than before.

Passing by people of every age and size, some of them give me curious looks, their gazes straying to the scythe in my hand. I leave the crowd behind to creep at the fringes. I glance from one stall to the next, awed by the variety of things offered at each table. Some of the pressure within me loosens, the heat in my chest cooling. So this... is what humans do.

My gaze narrows on Delilah standing at a booth where a woman hands her corn. The women say something to each other before Delilah grabs some napkins and walks away.

The woman at the booth stares after her, and when the woman's eyes land on me, I frown.

"Interested in some roasted corn or salsa?" she asks.

I've seen her before. She visited Sylvie on occasion.

Approaching, I wave my hand at the jars. "Do you make all of this yourself?"

"Most of it. But it's more of a hobby for me."

"A hobby?"

She eyes me like my question is strange. "Yes, a hobby. I grow most of my ingredients and purchase the rest locally."

"You enjoy farming?"

"I would say so. Is there something I could help you with?" she asks as I glance over the rest of her products. "Did you want to try a sample?"

"That woman you just gave corn to, she's selling Crow's Rest this fall."

"Yes, I heard..."

"I want to see it be purchased by someone..." I hesitate, trying to find the right word.

She crosses her arms. "I think I understand."

"I assume you and Sylvie were close?"

"Only in proximity."

The woman stares at me for a long moment.

"What's your name again?" she asks.

"My name's Jack. I've worked on the farm my entire life."

"I don't understand what you're getting after... Jack." She frowns at me. "What is it that you want?"

Isn't that obvious? "I want someone like you to buy the farm."

"Is that so?" She taps her chin. "It would have to be at a reasonable price. With the name it has, and the quality of its soil, as well as the acreage, it wouldn't be a bad investment."

"It's a deal then."

Flummoxed, her brows furrow as she goes back to staring at me. "Do others know it's going up for sale?"

"I don't believe so."

She laughs. When I smile back, she glances at my scythe. "You're an odd one Jack."

I bow my head. "I will try to do better next time."

She tilts her head and shifts her attention to the man standing behind me. I step aside and backtrack through the tents and toward the music.

I find Delilah by the stage with a drink in her hand, golden sun rays illuminating her relaxed form. The warmth in my chest returns, hotter than before, and with it, fractions of me stiffen while others loosen. My hands tense as my throat constricts. My lips part.

She is more than pretty.

She is... waving at someone. A man whom I've never seen before.

My mood shrivels and the airy feeling vanishes.

Chapter Fourteen

THE WARNING

Hollowstalk

Thick clouds blanket the sky. Around me people lift their hands, testing for rain. A cautious few gather their things.

When Delilah looks away from the male, disappointment slips over his face.

Her cheeks a blushing red, Delilah finishes her drink and tosses her cup in the garbage. She touches her brow as she faces the thunderclouds rolling in.

I glance at the male. He's still staring after her, and as I look around, I find others watching her too. They all notice my queen. My jaw clamps. I'm the one who works at her side, not them. Do they want to replace me? Do they see something I don't?

A thought takes root as I watch Delilah turn away from the crowd.

After the death of his mother, Ivar left in search of a queen, and that summer he brought home Sylvie. Before that, Ivar's mother also had a consort. Even the first queen had a companion. Someone who was always by her side.

Delilah did not show up with a partner.

Is she looking for one? I dismiss the thought. She doesn't need one. She has me. And besides, Sylvie was partnerless after Ivar's death. One is not needed.

I'm the one who is with her all day, and I don't need help.

My lips drop into a scowl, and I glare at those peering at her. It can't be that hard to frighten them, right? My hand clamps harder on my scythe.

Delilah, oblivious to my presence, leaves to thread through the parked vehicles.

Following her, I sneer at a male as I pass him by.

I stumble and brace against the nearest vehicle. Confused, I look down at my legs, finding them stiff. Lightning flashes as, to my horror, threads appear across the back of my hand.

I need to get back to the farm. Staggering to the road, my vision tunnels.

A strange emotion rushes through me as I stumble, catching my weight on my scythe. Excitement, anxiety, fear? I don't know. Whichever one it is, I don't like it, and I hurry along.

Crows circle my platform, and as I get closer, the air thickens with fear. For once, it does not make me giddy. The wind picks up, and the stalks bow under its might.

When I step onto the driveway, some of my strength returns.

As I approach the house, more crows flock to my platform. The lights are off. Where I expect to see a bike, there are only fireflies.

I hear a scream from the fields, and with it, the crows shriek and dive into the stalks.

Delilah.

I sprint into the corn. Crows pivot to peck at me, slowing me from reaching her. One wraps its claws around my arms, ripping my flesh. Weaving through the stalks, I spot my platform. The crows fly at Delilah from all sides, and she fights them off. Looming over it all is the Crow King's emissary.

"Get down!"

She answers with a cry and covers her head, dropping to her knees and crawling to the side of my platform. The crows continue to goad her as I dive forward and swing my scythe. The birds yowl and scatter as their emissary takes to the air and out of reach. I swing and feathers fill the air, swirling in a gust.

Delilah screams as she huddles, her arms over her head. I grab a bird tangled in her hair and throw the beast into the stalks. "Get to the house."

She doesn't seem to hear me, so I tug her into my chest and steer her toward the house. The crows chase after us, nipping our arms and legs. Sprinting to the porch, Delilah jerks out of my grip and lurches toward the front door. She digs into her purse.

I pivot, swiping at the bird. "Hurry."

"I'm trying!"

A shadow falls from above, large and wicked just as the rain begins to fall. The crows disperse as the shape wavers.

"Jack, the door's open!" Delilah calls out. "Get in here!"

The Crow King and I stare at one another for another second. "Jack! Get inside!"

I take one step back and then another, warning him away. His shadow regards me curiously.

Delilah tugs me inside. Slamming the door closed, she thumbs the lock into place as crows thump against the outside. Their shrill caws cut through the barrier with the wind and pelting rain.

Sliding down the door, Delilah covers her face with her hands, gasping for breath. Feathers stick out of her hair as blood drips down her skin. "What the hell... What the hell!"

I lean my scythe against the wall and kneel before her. She's covered in scratches. I'm wounded too, but unlike her, it is not blood pooling from me; instead, a sticky, clear substance clots the packed hay. I press a finger against a cut and am gifted a sharp sensation.

She exhales, brushing her hands over her wounds. "I don't know what happened. They were everywhere when I got home. I didn't know what to do. I tried to sneak past them through the stalks—" She shudders. "They were everywhere. Redeyes was waiting for me."

"Redeyes?"

"That big crow. That's what I call him."

Lightning flashes through the window as I stand. "I know which one you're referring to."

She tries to look up at me but cringes, jerking a hand to her neck. Covered in dirt and blood, a queen of mine has never looked more wrought.

"Let's get you upstairs." I wrap my arm under hers and pull her up. She releases a sharp gasp and a whimper.

I take her to her room, and she climbs into the bed, her hand cupping her forehead. My eyes dwell on the new air unit lodged in the window. A crow appears and pecks at the glass above it. Stomping over to it, I shove the curtains closed.

When I turn, Delilah is curled on her side and hugging a pillow.

Confused, I am at a loss for what I should do, and I search the room for an answer. When none appears, I pat my wet hair and clothes. I'm... miserable. Cold. Uncomfortable.

She must be miserable too.

I grab the folded blanket at the end of her bed and cover her.

"Thank you." She burrows deeper, her chin dipping under the cotton with a soft sigh. "The wine must have been stronger than I thought..."

By the time I get a good look at her face, her eyes are closed. Her hair is knotted, and her brow is scrunched and pale. I reach forward to brush the hair from her face and jerk my hand away, wondering what I'm doing.

My jaw clenches.

Only after seeing the Crow King, I'm worried too. Something must have sparked his attention...

I'd left out a portion of the raspberry harvest as a midsummer gift. And although it was an offering from me, I had believed it would be accepted.

I angered them.

And she paid for it.

Seeing her hurt like this, I question whether or not to tell her the truth. Testing her belief in such things did not go well earlier. She was not interested in hearing about her aunt's midsummer gift to the crows.

It's clear now that she is unaware.

But it might be too dangerous to explain to her what is at stake. Watching her settle further into sleep, I pull off my torn shirt and wipe the clear liquid trickling from my wounds.

It has to be enough that Delilah and I have the same goal, even if our reasons are different. I have everything under control.

Settling into the chair in the corner of the room, I pull thread and needle from my pocket and sew my wounds closed. When I'm done, I press my forehead against my hands and brood.

CHAPTER FIFTEEN

THIN THREADS

DELILAH

Uuugghh. I grip my head and groan.

My entire body hurts. My clothes tug against sensitive wounds, the fabric plastered to my skin. I'm sticky and sweaty. Throwing off the blanket, I curl my toes against the confines of my shoes.

With a sharp breath, I shuffle upright and stare down at the mess. Dried patches of blood dot my blankets and sheet—my dress as well. Dirt sticks to everything. I'm trying to make sense of it all when thunder rattles the window. Despite the clock reading midmorning, it's dark outside, and storm clouds paint the sky.

"You're awake."

My eyes snap to Jack standing in the doorway.

I startle at the sight of his bare chest—his very naked, very sculpted chest—and snatch my blanket closer. "Where is your shirt?"

"It's torn. I tossed it. Why?"

"I just..." I resist the urge to check him out as my traitorous gaze does so anyway. "I just wasn't expecting it. You surprised me, that's all." Shaking my head, my brows furrow. "Last night... You were there." I glance at his chest and arms, searching for wounds that aren't there. "I'm glad you didn't get hurt... I don't know what would have happened if you hadn't arrived. I don't know what set the crows off."

Suddenly it dawns on me that Jack is standing in my room—that he's in my house. A man I have only known for a month is half-dressed, looking like he belongs here. A man I find attractive even if there is something off about him.

I'm dirty, hurt, and wearing a torn dress. I don't know what makes me more nervous. Him or me. I can't stop looking at him, noticing he doesn't shy away from my perusal.

"Why *were* you out there?" I ask. He should've been home or at the festival—anywhere but the farm.

Jack tips his head and scans me slowly from head to toe.

Déjà vu hits, and for a second, I think it's... *Hollowstalk* standing before me. My anxiety spikes, rooting me in place.

He scans me again. "I was following you home."

"Following me home?"

"From the festival. I saw you leave."

"You were at the festival?"

He nods. "I saw you leave the farm and decided I would go too."

"I didn't see you there..." *Because I looked for you.*

He searches my gaze, answering slowly like his reason for following me should be obvious. "It was chaotic, and there were a lot of people."

"So you saw me leave and decided to follow? Why not go home?" Wondering if he has trailed me before, I clench the blanket closer.

"You left in the dark, right before a storm. It's a good thing I did because if I hadn't been there, you could have been hurt even worse."

I wince. "You followed me to make sure I got home safe?"

"Yes," he growls. Something like shock flashes over his face, but he quickly masks the reaction. And I feel it then, this strain between us, one I don't fully understand. A tension I think he might feel too.

My shoulders sag. If Jack were going to hurt me, he would've done it already. He'd had all night to do as he pleased.

And I yelled at him to get inside my house. I was the one who pulled him in.

Loosening my grip on the blanket, I sigh. "Sorry. I'm just anxious..." Feeling his eyes on me, I clear my throat and shuffle out of bed. "I'm going to clean up." There's dirt on him but no wounds. "You should clean up too, there's another bathroom downstairs if you haven't already found it. I'll be down shortly. Help yourself to coffee."

He steps into the hallway without complaint. Our eyes connect, holding for a moment as I close the door and lock it in place. Inhaling softly, I don't move until I hear the thrum of his footsteps on the stairs.

When I'm certain he's gone, I exhale, turn on my bedside lamp, and examine my ruined dress. Even if I could clean the dirt and bloodstains, there would be countless small tears. I shudder—still feeling the birds pecking me.

Rain blurs my view out the window and into the fields. In a flash, the clouds brighten with lightning. Thunder shakes the house.

I enter the bathroom, lock both doors, and set the shower to hot. Waiting for the water to heat up, I peel off the dress, careful where it sticks to my skin. After tossing it in the waste bin and downing two Ibuprofen, I step into the shower. The water stings as I wash around my wounds.

The crows attacked me unprovoked.

Crows don't do that... Right? I've heard they're smart and can hold grudges, but I didn't think they were dangerous.

By the time I step out of the shower, my skin is pruny and the bathroom is thick with steam. I take my sweet time bandaging my wounds, all to prolong the inevitable. Throwing on some sweatpants and a hoodie, I strip my bed and bundle it close, realizing I have nothing left to keep me here.

The house is quiet and dim when I finally make it downstairs. The drapes are closed, and the only light streams from the kitchen where several candles are burning. "Jack?" I look around.

"In here."

His voice comes from the office. Dropping my bedding off at the washer, I head for the converted den.

His back is toward me, his chest still bare, and the way his jeans hang dangerously low causes my heart to skip. His tousled hair drapes down his neck, drifting over his toned shoulders, and I reject the urge to touch them.

Sitting at the desk, he peers over the book at me.

I look sheepishly around the room. "I might have a shirt around here you can borrow..."

He shrugs. "I'm fine."

"You're not cold?"

"Cold? No. Not anymore." His eyes lift. "Are you?"

"I'm not."

Swallowing, uncertain of what to say and hating this stifled conversation, I peek at the book in his hand. "General Human Anatomy and Physiology? Interesting choice."

"I am searching for a way to heal your wounds. I don't think sewing them closed will help."

"I don't think I need stitches." Confused, I trace my fingers over my bandages. "I'll be fine. As long as nothing gets infected, they'll heal on their own. Besides, you're not going to find what you're looking for in that book."

He frowns. "I'm not?"

"No." I laugh. "That one is about how the human body works, not how to heal it."

He glances at the cover. "Oh."

Oh? "You didn't know that?"

"I didn't."

All the same, he grips the book, his forearm flexing. I try to see what page he's on but can't make out any details.

"Right." I swallow. "Well, is there someone who can pick you up? Do you need a ride? I don't think this weather is going to stop anytime soon."

"I don't, and I'm fine. You should rest."

I blink. "No one? There's no one who will miss you?"

"No."

"You've lived in the area all your life and you have no one?"

"No one."

"I didn't—"

He stands and strides over, cutting me off. When he stops directly before me, I look up as his gaze narrows on my face. Heat washes over me.

He scrutinizes me in silence.

Losing my nerve, I step back and cross my arms over my chest. "What are you doing?"

"I'm trying to figure out why I find you so distracting. Because right now, *Delilah*, I don't understand."

He pivots, and leaves the room, taking the book with him. He's gone before I can tell him I understand.

I understand all too well.

He never does set the anatomy book down, and even now, hours later, he's reading it at the dining room table while I wander the house searching for busy work. He watches me when he thinks I'm not looking. I feel his attention like an itch.

There's a strange familiarity in all of this, like we've done this before. Which doesn't make sense. We've never been in one another's company for this long, never this close, and never shared such a domestic environment.

I peer up at him, trailing my eyes over his relaxed form. "Do you want a sandwich?"

He turns a page. "No."

"Are you sure? I don't mind."

"I'm sure, Delilah. Focus on healing. I would prefer that is all you did."

"Why are you so focused on that book?" I nod at the anatomy text.

"The human body is far more intricate than I previously thought."

I cock my head. "You didn't have biology in high school?"

"No."

"But you did go to high school, right?"

Elmstitch is a small town, but it's not *that* small.

"Yes."

When he returns to his book, I cross my arms and exhale. He doesn't want me prying into personal matters. *Fine.*

"Do you know why the crows attacked?" I ask instead, unwilling to return to the awkward silence we've been sharing all day.

He leans back in his chair. "Do you *really* want to know?"

"Of course I do."

Jack shuts the book and stands. "They are afraid you won't keep them fed this winter."

"Fed?"

He walks across the room and begins to circle me. "If they are not given their due, the pact between you and the Crow King will be broken."

Crow King? It strikes me as crazy. But between curiosity and unease, I want to know more. "This pact, I've... read something about it. What is it exactly?"

"It's a payment for a blessing upon the land, a bargain of sorts."

"The crows attacked me because of this bargain?"

"Yes."

I swallow as he circles me again, forcing me to turn to keep him in my sight. "I've never made a pact with anyone, let alone with someone called the Crow King."

"You didn't, but others did on your behalf. Sylvie left the land to you and because of that, you also inherited it."

"That doesn't sound fair," I whisper. "That sounds like a curse, not a bargain."

He pauses. "Perhaps for some."

"So what happens if the pact is broken?"

"The land loses its blessing, the magic sustaining it fades, and you will have to answer to the Crow King."

I laugh. "All of this sounds ridiculous."

But Jack doesn't crack a smile and doesn't admit his act is up. Instead, his lips pinch in annoyance.

"You're serious, aren't you?"

Instead of answering, he leans closer and runs his thumb over a scrape on my cheek. I freeze at his touch. His face nears, his sharp features looming closer as his wide mouth hovers above my lips. My skin flushes.

He's going to kiss me.

I can imagine it—his mouth against mine, his hands running down my back.

He pulls away instead. "Yes, Delilah. I'm serious."

I jerk back, cheeks flushing crimson, and turn away so he doesn't see. "I don't appreciate being made fun of. You're prickly and opinionated, but I didn't think you were an asshole."

Without waiting for his reply, I return to my bedroom, angry that every guy I like turns out to be a jerk. But once I'm alone, I'm not sure if I'm more upset with Jack or myself for having risen to the bait.

Chapter Sixteen
SPROUTS

HOLLOWSTALK

The crows rest in the early July heat, lazily watching the new crop mature. Except for the emissary, they've left Delilah and me alone. They keep faith, at least so long as the summer heat drains their strength.

Walking through the rows, I count leaves, inspecting growth. The corn grows taller each day, the fields becoming lush and full.

These past few weeks since midsummer, I tend to the crops, and when that is done, I seek out Delilah, unable to keep away. She's become a tickle on the back of my neck or a loose thread threatening to unravel.

Watching the empty road, I'm increasingly aware that she still isn't back from her trip into town.

Ever since the storm, she confuses me more than ever, and I want to understand why. She is no different from any other human. Yet I respond in strange ways in her company, wanting to be near her—*needing* to be near her.

Unfortunately, the anatomy book gave me more questions than answers. It helped me realize that though I may appear human, I'm not human at all. My body is packed with straw and hay and the bones of crows. Whereas humans have nerves, muscles, blood, and so much more... And that's on the inside. Externally, I don't even have all the appendages humans have—I don't have a cock.

I look down at the flat crotch of my pants. A cock is the one limb I'm missing.

But what need would I have for one?

Human males have cocks so they can penetrate and copulate with their female counterparts. The text says this act is something intimate partners share. It may explain why Delilah waved to the male at the festival. If she is interested in having a partner, she would expect this type of interaction.

This new knowledge excites me. The more I'm near her, the more I imagine what a union between us would be like, if she would ever let me have access to her body. The book says it is pleasurable, and perhaps my pleasuring of her will steer her eyes toward me and away from others.

Has she already expressed this interest in me—have I acted untoward to her? There are many cues I may have missed.

I strain my ears, listening for her truck to rumble down the dirt road, but all I hear are crickets.

I should have gone with her. My jaw ticks as I stretch my stiff fingers. This longing is not a sensation I enjoy. It has become obsessive—this idea of us being partners, and when I hear the sound of a vehicle, I battle the urge to greet her, asking if she'd like me to have a cock so I might penetrate her.

However, when I reach the front yard, Delilah's truck is nowhere to be found. Instead, there's a strange car parked out front.

When I catch sight of a woman at the wheel, recognition crosses my mind. *The woman with the corn. Miranda.* Torn between retreat and approach, Delilah pulls up behind her and parks.

Curious, I linger in the stalks.

Delilah jumps down from the truck and smiles. "Well, this is it." She waves toward the house. "What do you think?"

"It's lovely."

The two of them begin to circle the exterior.

"I still need to have the house painted," Delilah adds.

"Of course, of course."

"Central air will be installed in a couple of weeks. There's a new water heater on backorder. Everything will be done by the fall."

Miranda puts a hand on Delilah's shoulder. "Relax. You're doing great. I'm impressed."

Delilah eases, her smile brightening. "Would you like to see the inside of the house?"

"Absolutely."

As Delilah leads Miranda away, my annoyance grows. It shouldn't, but it does. Her visit is a good thing. It means she's considering the proposal.

I creep closer to the house, hoping to hear more of what Delilah has to say. But upon seeing Miranda's reflection in the window, I scowl. Waiting for them to come back out, I linger nearby. A few minutes later, Delilah walks Miranda to her car.

Miranda lowers into her vehicle. "The place really is lovely. It would make your aunt proud."

She drives off as Delilah watches from the deck.

Miranda may be the next queen, but I am not done with Delilah, not anymore.

I wonder if Miranda has a partner already and if she doesn't, would she consider me? The thought recoils me, imagining she and I as close as I imagine being with Delilah. As much as my head is consumed by the predicament Delilah has caused me, I enjoy her company.

The heat in my chest rises anew, and I press my hand to it in the hopes of rubbing the sensation away. These days, it warms more and more often.

Peering between the stalks of corn, I watch her. She stretches, rubs her brow, and strides back into the house. I stare after her long after she's gone.

The afternoon comes and goes, and she doesn't come back out.

When dusk begins to settle, I decide to call it a day and head for my platform. Crawling beneath the boards, I lie on my back. The sky darkens through the wood slats above me, and as I'm about to close my eyes, a large shadow blocks the remaining light.

"You waste your strength on trivial matters," the Crow King scolds. "She must be made aware." The details of his face and body are irresolute and obscured.

"What does it matter? She is planning to sell the land."

"The offering is meant to be from a human, not you," he warns. "Your interpretation of the pact stretches its intentions."

"Why not me? If I can remain as I am and take ownership, your minions will never have to worry about going hungry again. There would be a harvest every year."

"It is an unsustainable plan. You are bound to this world by fragments as it is. You know this."

I do know, and I find it increasingly unfair.

I like my freedom.

I want to keep it.

"I don't care who is queen, and nor should you, as long as there is a human. We can only take from their world what is promised," he continues. "She is to feed my crows, and if she doesn't, she will be punished."

I hesitate. "What if a human can be more?"

He scoffs. "Poor scarecrow. You have spent too long in this world." His shadow darkens. "Ensure there is a harvest, even if she is unaware. Otherwise, my blessing will leave this place, in search of someone else who will celebrate it. The last time I was denied, the farm was only spared out of my good grace. On a second offense, I will not be so kind."

He fades away, the threat lingering in his wake, and I know there's little in my power to stop him.

CHAPTER SEVENTEEN

WINIFRED AND HOLLOWSTALK

DELILAH

I check my supplies and inspect the white sheets draped around me. It's time to trash the old floral wallpaper so I can paint the interior of the house. I've procrastinated long enough. Thankfully, the relentless heat of early July has ebbed, and a cool snap has dropped the temperature to humane levels.

I pick up my water bottle and take a long swig. I have a potential buyer, and of all people, it's the lady from the festival, Miranda. There's nothing official, nothing documented, though she and I have talked a lot over the last couple of weeks. She is far more passionate about crops than I am.

Jack would prefer someone like her. I think. Miranda would hire him for help, I'm certain of it. He's handy and strong, he's knowledgeable about the land and knows how to work the equipment. He's great to have around even if he's often surly.

I haven't told him about Miranda yet, and I don't think I will until I have an official offer, which is hopefully soon. I don't want to raise his hopes that he might get to say goodbye to me earlier than expected.

Glancing out the window, I watch as he opens the back barn's doors.

I was certain he was going to kiss me.

He didn't, and ever since, I've felt like an idiot. Being around him makes me jumpy and my stomach flip. I hate it. Squeezing my eyes closed, I will my crush on Jack to go away. It's embarrassing. I don't know what has gotten into me.

Stupid, annoying hormones.

He believes in magical pacts and strange gods.

It's ridiculous. It's unusual. When I first met him, he seemed normal enough. But Aunt Sylvie believed in this stuff too, and she wasn't crazy. Just eccentric.

Maybe they're members of a cult. I let out a laugh. *The Cult of the Crow King.*

Except, like Jack, I still want to know why Aunt Sylvie left me this place. I want to know what she was thinking when she made me, a niece she barely knew, her inheritor. I'd assumed she left me everything because I was her best option within the family. Now I'm not so sure.

Soaking the wallpaper and using a scraper to lift an edge, I tear a large piece away.

My phone rings when I'm just getting into the groove, and I scoff, seeing my brother's name on the screen. I strip off a glove and pick it up. "I'm busy."

"Yeah, I know," Daniel mutters. "But you need to hear this."

"Hear what?"

"Mom was browsing the website of that athletic club you work at, and there's a job listing. One that's identical to your position."

The last time I talked to my boss was over a month ago. *Shit.* "I'll deal with it."

"Good."

"And you better tell Mom off for snooping."

"She's just worried. If something does happen—"

I squeeze my phone. "I have a potential buyer. I'll be done on time."

"Oh?"

"Yeah. So I have a lot of work to do."

"Fine. But if anything goes wrong—"

"Stop doubting me."

I hang up and groan. My parents can't imagine their princess not moving back home, marrying some rich guy from their club, and quitting her job to raise a bunch of babies. Mom wants one more thing to brag about to her friends, and the fact that she's using Daniel to keep tabs on me hasn't been ignored.

I don't *need* a guy. Or money. Or status. And I especially don't want to be around people who will judge me all the time.

Wetting another section of wallpaper, I tear it down.

The next section sticks. I use my scraper to move it along, but it clicks, striking metal. Curious, I scrape it again and get the same click. I run my fingers against the anomaly, discovering a subtle bulge behind the wallpaper. It's rectangular, about the height of my hand, and twice as wide. Wary of anything electrical, I clear the remaining wallpaper around it.

When I'm done, I discover a recessed steel box with a little hole in the center of it.

I grab a flashlight to peer inside.

Two eyes glint back at me.

I rear away. Across the room, I stare at the box as if a monster is about to crash through the wall and tear me apart. When seconds pass and nothing happens, I tiptoe closer and take another peek.

It's a crow's skull, not a ghoul.

There's nothing to be afraid of.

I slip my finger into the hole and pull. The box gives way and I totter under its weight, holding back a sneeze as dust blasts my face.

Carefully setting the box down, I open the top and examine its contents: the skull and a leather journal. The journal is old, the pages yellowed, and the binding cracks as I open the cover.

On the first page is a name written in intricate cursive, *Winifred Merriweather, Queen.*

Queen. That word again.

The skull looks like the one Hollowstalk wore.

Sitting back, I gently open the book and begin to read. It's a grimoire of sorts, with sections dedicated to a large range of topics including a list of coven meetings sorted by date, detailing attempted spells and their result. They discuss common concerns—rituals for rain, childbirth, and healing.

It's the final section that draws me in. It's a manifesto, a collection of journal entries about something called *Winifred's Bargain.* Clearly, Aunt Sylvie's obsession with corn wasn't the first.

On the next page, I find a sketch of...

Hollowstalk.

I grip the cover and read every word. I learn the shape of every burlap and leather piece that composed his form and that his hair was plucked from a horse's tail. He was packed with both hay and straw and the bones of dead crows.

It took her over a month to finish him, and the project nearly killed her. She didn't write how.

There's a page entitled *The Pact.* Scanning quickly, I see a reference to a Crow King and an offering to the crows.

My heart is pounding by the time I reach the end and find a page titled *Queens of Crow's Rest*. Winifred has written each name in full and most are paired with a signature at its side.

I put the book down and retrieve my aunt's timeline from her desk and compare the names to the previous owners. They match.

Except for the last line.

At the bottom of the page, beneath Sylvie's printed name, another name is scrawled in Winifred's hand, *Delilah Rose Mackey*, the signature line left blank.

Desperate to make sense of this, several minutes pass before I manage to trek to the kitchen for a glass of water.

When I glance out the window, Redeyes is there.

I squeeze my eyes closed and grip the counter. Lightheadedness crowds my head as doubt fills me. Turning away, I drink my water. When I face the window again, Jack is there, walking out of the barn. Not wanting him to see me, I retreat to the den. Hands shaking, I put the book to the side and get back to work.

CHAPTER EIGHTEEN

THE FIRST KISS

DELILAH

That evening, I pace downstairs, keeping an eye on Jack as he fiddles with one of the sprinklers in the backyard. The day is late and reds paint the sky. Fat white clouds are haloed in gold, catching the last beams of light.

He'll be heading home soon.

For the hundredth time, he looks up, and I duck away from the window. He's been doing this all afternoon, ever since I started keeping tabs on him. He could've been checking on me for weeks, and I wouldn't have known. I only started stalking him a couple of hours ago.

Whatever his reason for looking for me—because who else would he be searching for—doesn't bother me as much as it probably should. He's never hurt me. He might be in league with a "crow god," but that doesn't make him dangerous.

It makes him interesting.

When his attention is back on the broken sprinkler, I shift from my hiding spot. As the sky turns a dusky purple, I quietly open the front door and sneak out. Crouched in the bushes beside the house, I wait for Jack to finish for the day.

I don't have to wait long. Standing, he takes off his gloves and stuffs them into his back pocket. Hauling the sprinkler into the barn, he covers it with a tarp before shutting the door and locking it with a chain. When he's done, he turns toward the house.

I slink deeper into the bushes.

He stares in my direction, but his gaze doesn't land. My heart thrums, wondering if he really *is* looking for me...

The flood lights click on, brightening his sharp features. With a breeze, his clothes press against him, contouring to his muscled frame. As the sky darkens and he continues to stare at the house, I frown, losing courage, and wonder if I should make myself known.

He doesn't talk about home. He says he has no one. I want to know where he goes.

He knows things that were mentioned in Winifred's journal. A journal that was hidden in a wall.

Finally, his gaze drops, and he grabs his scythe. I hold my breath as he passes me. When he crosses the front yard, I creep after him. At the end of the driveway, he turns left when I expect him to take a right.

Left is a dead end. There's nothing except forest that way.

Quickening my step, I peek through the stalks after him. Where the road ends at the edge of the farm, he keeps going, vanishing into the trees. When I reach the spot where he disappeared, I peer into the shadows, searching for a trail. There's none.

Instead, I hear a splash. Hearing another, I crouch and enter the forest, heading toward the sound.

After a few steps, I reach a clearing with a brook. Running parallel to the fields, a stream flows out of sight in both directions. It's large enough to swim in and bordered by bushes and grass. Wildflowers sprout along its banks.

To my left, I spy Jack's scythe leaning against a tree. Past it, a shirtless Jack kneels next to the water.

I freeze.

He dips and wrings out a cloth before shaking it open and spreading it on the grass to dry. Afterward, he leans over the water and scoops it into his hands, splashing his face and chest, and rinsing his neck and arms.

As water trickles down his skin, he leans back and looks up at the moon. "I know you're there, Delilah."

I jump. "I wasn't following—well, I was following you, but it's not what it seems. You see—" I take a deep breath, unable to hold back a long-winded explanation. "I wanted to know where you go, and well, one thing led to another. It spiraled out of control. So there. You caught me. Fuck." My face is inflamed by the time I'm done. I bury it in my palms and groan.

When I next look up, he's walking toward me.

"I'm really sorry, Jack. I shouldn't have invaded your privacy—" I choke on my words.

He stops a little too close, his gaze narrowed. "Why are you flustered?"

My eyes dip to his chest. "Because you're half naked!"

I sag in defeat, increasingly mortified with every passing second. Especially since he's assessing me in that silent way of his.

"You shouldn't be out here at night."

My mouth opens then shuts, then opens again. "Why?"

"It's dangerous. It's easy to trip and get hurt. Cougars and wolves pass through, and the crows roost here when the sun sets."

"Why are you out here then?"

"I like the forest."

I squint. "When it's so dangerous?"

He takes another short step closer. "I've tried to tell you, but you didn't want to listen. It should not have had to come from me. I'm just a product of all of this."

"The pact?" I prompt. "You're talking about the pact."

"You don't need to worry about that."

"I don't?"

He lifts a finger to my cheek and sweeps a strand of my hair behind my ear. "I'm taking care of it."

Shivering from his touch, I close my eyes. I shouldn't have followed him out here.

I turn away. "I'm going to go."

He grabs my arm and stops me. Peering up at him, I meet his gaze—sharp and heated.

"Delilah." He murmurs my name, his low voice sending shivers up my spine. "I have something to tell you."

My heart stutters. "Y-you do?"

He leans into me and loosens his hold on my arm, his fingertips trailing upward. "I want to be closer to you, my queen. More than anything, I want this."

Queen.

I rest my hand on his chest.

He tenses and looks down.

Beneath my fingers, his skin is soft and smooth.

Shyly I begin to lift away when he snatches my hand with both of his. He presses my palm back into place and slides his hands up my arm, over my shoulders, neck, and face, to fist into my hair. My scalp prickles, aware of every little thing he does as he leans his mouth closer to mine.

"Yes." He stops a hairsbreadth from my lips. "What now?"

It sounds like a taunt. I jerk up and press my mouth to his. Firm at first, his lips part at my strike. I coax and taunt him back, demanding he make the next move before I get my head on straight.

When he doesn't, I pull away.

His fingers cling to my hair as he tugs me back into him. His lips land on my cheek and part against my skin, breathing me in. They drift down, along my jaw, inhaling the whole way. "Delilah." Jack tugs my head back to take his next breath against my neck.

I squirm, breathless, undone by the way his voice roughens saying my name. His hands keep me captive, weaved into my hair, as his mouth lowers, exploring the skin above my shirt.

I want to back away. A pent-up part of me is taut with need.

He glides his mouth up my throat, along the curve of my cheek, and over my hairline. Grabbing his face, I capture his mouth once more. He stills as I shift my lips against his. Unsure why he doesn't kiss me back, I slide my hands down his chest.

My fingers find rough patches I hadn't noticed before.

When he remains frozen, I open my eyes to look at him. "Jack, have you ever kissed a girl before?"

"No."

I release a breathy laugh. "That wasn't what I was expecting. I don't think I can believe anything you say."

"Then don't think."

"Then you should kiss me."

I weave my fingers into his hair, mirroring his hold on me, and gently press my mouth back to his. He gives way, letting me set the pace. In the dark, my courage grows.

I tease him with the tip of my tongue and nibble his lower lip. All the while, he holds me tight, like he's afraid I'll stop if he doesn't. It's a little too strong, a little too rough.

He hums when I nip his lip again, gauging his reaction, and he nips mine back. My tongue presses his, and he does the same. Whatever I do, he mimics, and the little game eases any remaining doubts.

Maybe he really hasn't kissed a girl before.

His mouth stalls, and he pulls back. His gaze narrows on my face.

Confused, my brow furrows. "Jack?"

Suddenly he shoves his mouth down on mine, his lips frantic. I gasp, shocked by the sudden change. Grabbing him, my hand moves down his back as he yanks me against him.

One of my fingers catches on something in his skin. A string?

Tugging my hand away, something like a thread comes with it, and I shake it off. When I return my hand to Jack, it lands on something rough with sharp ends that poke me.

I wrap my fingers around it, confused. Pulling at it, a growing tangle of strings and detritus collects in my hand. Jack jerks away, trying to look at his back, and I become even more confused.

"Are you okay?" There's a large burlap patch on his back with hay sticking out. Squinting, I try to see how it's attached, but it's too dark. "What's on your back?"

He throws out his arm when I try to move closer. "Stay away from me," he warns. Striding to the stream, he snatches his damp shirt off the ground, pulls it on, and grabs his scythe.

I head straight for him. "I don't understand what's going on."

What the hell was that?

He turns on me with a scowl. "Do not follow me out here again." The vehemence in his tone stuns me. Pivoting, he storms into the forest.

There's an urge to shout after him, but I have no idea what to say. I feel betrayed, more confused than ever, and angry. I look around, trying to make sense of where everything went wrong. Hugging my arms to my chest, I eye the long shadows that blend into the darkness of night. Shame pits in my stomach. By coming out here, I've made everything more complicated.

And I know even less than I did before.

Finally looking at what's in my hand, I find a clump of dry, brittle hay and a tangle of string clenched between my fingers.

I hear the flap of wings, and stiffening with fear, I wait for the sound to pass. Pocketing the hay and string, I'm certain now that Jack isn't coming back.

Hurt, I head home.

CHAPTER NINETEEN

THE PAST

DELILAH

For the next few days, I avoid Jack.

Which is easy because he's been avoiding me too. At first, I hoped he would find me and explain what happened, but he didn't, and now that it's been days, I don't think he will.

I close my eyes and chew on my bottom lip, torn by it all.

Turning over the hay one more time, I hide it with the journal, the second crow skull, and the timeline in my bedside drawer. To keep busy, and avoid asking Jack again about it, I've compiled everything I've found on the pact.

So far, the journal is my best source of information. I'm hoping somewhere in its pages is an explanation that will make some sort of sense.

As far as I know, the farm is blessed by this Crow King, and that blessing ensures the soil is rich, perhaps magical. In turn, the Crow King and his subjects receive half of the crop grown from it—with a minimum amount to guarantee the crows are fed through the winter. This tribute is due by Samhain, or Halloween, but can be given prior. In exchange, the human who owns and works the land—the pactholder—will have *prosperity*.

It's simple enough, a symbiotic exchange. Not terribly crazy. There are countless stories about people receiving godly blessings and humans working with animals.

Winifred started it all in 1823.

Whoever owns the farm takes on the agreement. Winifred calls women pactholders "queens" to satisfy her 1820s feminist humor while the men are simply *pactholders*. How everyone prospered isn't clear, but I infer the previous owners sold their portion of the harvest to make an income. From other records, I know selling seeds from the produce grown here has made the most.

Crow's Rest once supplied seeds all around the world, but according to my aunt's paperwork, she pulled back from that part of the business years ago, focusing more on the local market—and placing in the state fair.

Her income wasn't outrageous, although it was sustainable. Her tools and machines were state of the art at their time of purchase and to this day are in great condition according to Jack. But it's hard to believe the money was worth it.

I inherited a little more than fifty thousand dollars—just enough to fix up the place. She wasn't rich by any means. So why did she bother? And why give it all to me? Why not leave and retire?

And why is Jack asking these questions too? What does he know that I don't?

He knows more than I do, and that doesn't make sense. What does he get from all of this? Groaning, I press my fingers to my temples.

I keep turning pages until I reach the back. Glancing at the spot where my name is inscribed in Winifred's hand, I slam the book shut.

A short time later, I head out to my truck to unload it. Inside the bed are the supplies I bought for today's project.

Now the crops are ripening, the crows pick apart the immature cobs, leaving a mess wherever they go. So I need a new scarecrow. Only this one will be of my own making and far less creepy than Hollowstalk.

I'm getting paranoid, and now more than ever, I want to sell this place to Miranda.

She's a nice lady, and she'd be happy here. She'd have ample produce to sell at the festivals and farmer's markets. She'd have a cozy house, privacy, and land.

Beautiful land.

I look over the flowers around the house, the new fence, the barns, and out over the fields. *She'll have gorgeous land...*

Carrying the supplies to the back barn, I nudge the double doors open with my hip. Setting down my load, I drag a folded table into the open doorway and spread everything out. Burlap, needles, yarn, tattered clothes from a local thrift shop, and my hot glue gun. Inventorying my goodies, I hope to god I can make this work.

I scan the fields, hoping Jack will notice that I'm outside today. He continues to avoid me, and I'm over it. I can't fix anything if he's avoiding me.

Jack visits the back barn at least once each day, so if I wait long enough, I'm bound to see him.

Unraveling an extension cord, I plug in my glue gun and add batteries to the radio I splurged on. Dialing through the stations, I land on one playing classic rock.

Revving up to the voice of Tom Petty, I get ready to create the coolest scarecrow this farm has ever seen.

I quickly dismiss my foldout table for the grass, scattering everywhere, and begin by nailing together a tall cross out of wood beams. Going to the burlap next, I brainstorm patterns and how I should cut the pieces. Only it's harder to cut than I thought, and the edges turn out jagged and frayed.

I get a little creative—desperate maybe—with how I use the tools at my disposal. What I thought was going to be a fun craft project turns into an exhaustive task of nailing, gluing, and stapling materials that don't want to stick together.

By midday, all I have to show for my work is a huge mess of cut cloth, sticky string, and a loose pile of straw.

Determined to conquer scarecrow making, I shift tactics and lean the cross that's supposed to be the scarecrow's body against the barn wall.

Clutching a deformed ball of burlap, sporting black ribbons of glued-on hair and a face that sags no matter how much straw I stuff inside it, I stake the head on the top of the pole and tie off the bottom hole. Stepping back, I grimace.

The eyes are off-center, and the hair is uneven in a way that can only be described as horrific. Hot glue strings stick out everywhere. It's worse than I could've imagined.

It's awful and the creepiest thing I've ever seen.

I now have a greater appreciation for Winifred's skill in creating Hollowstalk. She had a talent I can barely fathom.

Annoyed, I snatch an old denim jacket from my supplies and shove it over the scarecrow's wooden arms. It hangs dejectedly on the frame.

Defeated, I look around to see what I can use to make it better only to be frustrated by the mess I've made and the time I've wasted.

Deciding it's time for a break, I sulk to the house's back entrance and pour a cup of lemonade from a pitcher in the fridge. Once I have a semblance of patience and a large bundle of dirty sheets collected in my arms, I head back out with a new plan in mind.

Jack is there when I return, leaning against his scythe and staring at my deformed scarecrow.

My feet falter.

Collecting myself, I walk up to stand beside him. "Hi."

He doesn't look at me. "Hi."

"I haven't seen you the last few days. Are..." I lick my lips. "Are you okay? I'm really sorry about the other night."

"What is this?" he asks like he doesn't hear me, indicating my shameful creation.

"I was trying to make a new scarecrow."

He glances at me. "You're making a scarecrow..." His face hardens, and his lips flatten, strained and tense. "A new one?"

"I thought it would be fun. The platform in the front field has been empty since I tossed the last one," I tell him when I really mean: *I came up with a bullshit excuse to be in the barn all day so I can talk to you.* "Look, I've been meaning to catch you—"

He turns away, taking in the supplies strewn everywhere. He slowly wanders through them, sometimes picking something up, and testing it in his hands before placing it back down. "Sticks, cloth, glue, nails, wood, and plastic," he mutters like he's annoyed, snatching up a cheap cowboy hat. "You think you can replace Hollowstalk with *this?*"

I sigh deeply. "What else would I use?"

"Nothing!" He turns on me. "You don't need another scarecrow. You've got me."

I laugh. "You're not a scarecrow, Jack." I drop my bundle and sigh again. "Look, it hasn't been fun at all. But I've been scraping wallpaper down for days, and I needed a break. Also... I wanted to talk to you about the other night."

"The other night was a mistake."

He says it with such nonchalant finality that I frown, taken aback.

Swallowing, I force myself to agree with him, trying not to let his words hurt me. "It was. You're right. It won't happen again." I swallow my disappointment. I don't want him to see me upset.

"Do you..." I hesitate, suddenly nervous around him, as if speaking about the pact, pretending it's real long enough to ask questions, might make it so, but even if he wants nothing to do with me beyond the farm, I want him to know I'm ready to hear what he has to say about it. "Do you have any guesses why my aunt might have left everything to me?"

He's silent for a long stretch, and I think he's not going to answer me, but then he levels with me. "I wish I did. It was her responsibility to ensure her heir was prepared. Perhaps she simply thought she would live longer and would have more time."

"I see." I search my memory, recalling Sylvie's final visit to California several years ago. She'd gotten into a fight with my dad for lighting incense and causing him to have an asthma attack. She left afterward and didn't come back.

"If you're going to make a new one, show me how you're doing it. Maybe I can help."

"The scarecrow?"

"Yes."

"Oh... Okay. Sure. But humor me, what changed your mind?"

He kneels in front of the pole and runs his hand up the wood. "The anatomy is off."

I step forward to show him what I've done so far, wishing I could read him better. "I made a head and a cross for his body, and well, that's all I've accomplished so far. I still need to finish his limbs, bulk him up with straw, and dress him. His face is so creepy..." I cringe.

"The face is promising. It's scary."

"Is that an insult?"

"It's a compliment. He should be terrifying."

"That's the thing though, I don't want him to be frightening. Hollowstalk was scary, and that's why I got rid of him. One night, and you'll find this funny because it is, I swore he moved. I'd dumped him the day before, and that night, it was strange... The next morning, he was back up on his pole. I still can't make sense of it. I don't think I ever will."

He slants his eyes at me. "It sounds like Hollowstalk wanted to scare you. Maybe he didn't like being thrown out."

"Yeah, well, he was just a sewn sack of hay, so he didn't have a choice. Though... I guess he wins after all. So there's that."

Jack stands and faces me. "He does?"

"The crows were worse afterward. You know that." I watch his expression, waiting to see if he'll argue, but to my surprise, he looks intrigued.

Sliding his gaze over me once, he turns back to the scarecrow, his interest piquing. "Tell me how I can help."

"Sure."

I explain what I'd hoped to achieve. Jack stays attentive, sorting through the materials on the table and floor. He gathers a pile of cloth, scissors, needles, and yarn, before sitting cross-legged on the ground. Taking hold of the scissors, he cuts into the cloth.

I take the head off of the pole and sit across from him, watching him through my lashes as I finetune the face.

Jack is meticulous in how he sews the limbs together, each puncture of his needle precise and perfect. When I'm done, feeling awkward with nothing to do, I dash inside to make us food.

It's evening by the time Jack is putting on the finishing touches, and the dinner I made is still untouched beside him.

He hovers over the scarecrow's body, making it hard for me to see what he's working on. I decide to take his dinner into the fridge, and when I'm back, he stands, carries it to the pole, and attaches the body to it. Excited that it's finally done, I join him, picking up the cowboy hat along the way.

In the simple shape of a human, the scarecrow now has his form, his contours clean and proportionate.

The same goes for the large cock with a bulging middle hanging between his two cylindrical legs.

A cock. He gave my scarecrow a cock.

Stunned silent, I stare at the appendage as Jack attaches the head back to the top.

He sewed a cock onto the scarecrow.

And I didn't even notice. Yet, clear as day, a cock juts out between the scarecrow's legs, framed by two firm balls.

I take a step back and look between Jack and the scarecrow's dick. Giving nothing away, like the cock isn't unusual at all, he finishes attaching the scarecrow to the pole.

"So, question." I purse my lips, wondering why every situation with him is weirder than the last. "Why the cock?"

"Because he's a male. You said so yourself."

"So?"

"Males have cocks. And testes." He straightens and looks at me, his face half in shadow. "Is something wrong?"

"No... I'm just trying to understand."

Jack shrugs like sewing a large cock on a scarecrow is the most normal thing in the world. "He should have the relevant anatomy."

"He's a scarecrow!"

"Is there something wrong with that?"

"Really? Jack, really? You're crazy, you know that, right?"

"I do now." He frowns.

"I didn't mean—"

He puts up a hand. "Is the cock a problem or not, Delilah?" His gaze narrows on me like the answer is important, more important than *why* he sewed a cock onto my scarecrow in the first place.

I swallow.

With his eyes searing my flesh, urging me for an answer, I cross my arms and scrunch my face. If this is his way of flirting... "Stop it."

He searches my face. "Stop what?"

"Whatever this is you're doing!"

His brow furrows like he has no idea what I'm talking about—which is very like him. He sighs, quiets his voice, and points to the cock. "So, is it a problem or not?"

I throw up my arms, unable to tell if he's playing with me. I think that's what has confused me about him this entire time. He's clearly a grown man and mature, although clearly with proclivities, but he also comes off innocent which are two things that don't go together.

Has he really never kissed anyone before me? Does he really know nothing about the human body? His body? Does he truly think it's appropriate to put a cock on my scarecrow?

Or is this all some sort of joke to him?

I should turn on my heel and leave.

But I don't—I study his expression, knowing the answer is there, I just have to look closely enough. Glancing back at the scarecrow, I have to admit the cock doesn't seem entirely out of place. My issue is that it's *Jack* doing this.

When I look back at him, he smiles slowly. "You're okay with it. You like cock."

I guffaw. "You're absurd. Has anyone told you that?"

He's nothing like anyone else. He's not boring or predictable, vain, or pompous—he has nothing to prove and he doesn't care. Being in his company is how I always wished my family could be. Instead, at the smallest act of nonconformance, they scold me. My late aunt was the one exception, and she left.

For once, I'm free to do the strange thing. To have a scarecrow with a cock.

I size up the large appendage and smile. "You're right, I do like it. I'm more than okay with it. In fact, it's great because my parents would hate it, which makes me like it even more."

My answer makes him grin.

It's the type of smile that strikes straight to my core despite his absurdity, an image that sticks with me for the rest of the day.

Later that night in bed, I slip my hand into my panties and thrum my clit, eager to stop aching.

I don't want to think of Jack.

I don't mean to think of Jack.

But the way he rubbed his mouth all over me by the stream incites my fingers to rub faster. I can see him shirtless, standing over me, watching my hand move, watching it like it's the most fascinating thing he's ever seen—my fingers pleasuring my pussy.

I'm haughty, unafraid to show him what he wants to see, and I run my finger along myself, spreading my arousal, just to see what he will do. In response, he stares with fixed awe, his lips twisting into a hungry smile. Smirking in response, I push my finger inside myself and look down at his cock.

His jeans hang indecently low, the vee of his hips leading toward a tent in the fabric big enough to be the scarecrow's cock. I tug at his waistband, lowering it down until—

I snap, hips rocking, gasping out as my orgasm strikes. I writhe in my sheets, riding out the waves possessing my body. As I catch my breath and settle, disappointment sets in.

I curse, turn over in bed, and bury my head in my pillow.

Chapter Twenty

Anatomy Lesson

I pace the barn in the dark. There's a tightening in my stomach. The skin around my stitching aches as a salty taste fills my mouth.

She nearly discovered me by the stream. She dug her fingers into my body and tugged out hay—*my* hay.

I almost turned back into a scarecrow before her eyes.

My jaw ticks as I look at the scarecrow we made today. So small and simple compared to me. This is my fate should I fade.

A fate I will do anything to avoid now that I know what I've been missing. I run my fingers over my lips. My queen kissed me, and it's all I think about. I didn't want it to end.

Having Delilah in my arms soothed the ache in my chest—for a tantalizing moment, her lips helped me forget that I'm not human, that I'm only pretending. I want her to want me so I might touch her.

She thinks I'm crazy, that I act strange. Which means I'm not doing as good of a job pretending to be human as I thought I was.

Sliding the barn door open, I let in the moonlight and look up at her window. For a moment, the pane is bright, and then she clicks off her light.

I retrieve the needle and yarn from earlier and drop them beside the new scarecrow. Dragging over a stool from the back workstation, I snatch the scissors on the table and seize the scarecrow's cock.

I learned something important today.

Delilah likes cock.

Cutting it off, I clear the broken threads. Turning the coarse phallic shape in my hands, I get used to holding it.

Using the scissors, I slice into the middle of the appendage, opening it up. Next, I dig its point into my arm and carefully score across. My skin turns, becoming that of a scarecrow as tufts of hay, straw, and bits of bone bulge out of the rip. I sift my fingers through my stuffing and remove a handful.

I push the material into the cock. By the time it's packed tight, it's bigger, longer than before, the middle bulging more than ever, and I have to patch it with extra cloth.

When I finish tying the last string and sealing the appendage, it warms in my hands, stiff and full. Taut. Easy to handle. The balls are firmer now, softening out with added material. The tip ends in a smooth curve, and the middle is wide and girthy, perhaps a little more than is necessary.

All I have left now is to attach it.

Sitting back, I peer up at Delilah's window again.

Unbuttoning my jeans, I shove them down my legs. Tracing her window with my eyes, I spread my thighs and press the edge of the scissors into my coarse flesh. Hay pops out in a hefty tuft. Pressing it aside, I pick up the cock and compress the large phallic shape against my once smooth groin. Nerves spark as my strings shift and my body claims the addition.

Squeezing my eyes shut, I groan.

Delilah.

A mystifying sensation tightens the cock as it finishes connecting with my body. It quickly intermingles with the raging inferno building within my chest, and my fingers scrape over my body searching for the flames, desperate to put them out.

Little by little, the heat ebbs, allowing me to think. Gritting through the discomfort, I lower my hands and hold still, waiting for it to pass. When it's gone, I grab the needle and yarn and start to sew.

Securing the cock isn't as easy as I hoped. Adding a new limb is taxing in a way I never thought possible. Every jab of the needle shocks me, stopping my hand mid-puncture. The resulting line is wavy, and disjointed because my fingers won't stop shuddering. Heaving, I finish the job. Patching up my arm, the needle drops from my fingers as I rest my elbows on my knees.

By the time I can think clearly again, there's a mess of straw, cloth, and yarn pooled around my feet.

Tense, I sit upright and roll my neck. I feel out the cock, gripping it in my fist.

It's hotter than fire and more sensitive than any other part of me. Rubbing it, the textured patchwork fades into soft, human skin. Veins appear, popping out as I check it over. The more I touch it, the more responsive it becomes.

The tip forms into a mushroom, and when my grip tightens, I moan with pleasure. Squeezing it against the cup of my hand, the pleasure builds. Liking the feeling a little too much, I jerk my hand faster, squeezing harder, testing how far the pleasure will go as an image of Delilah in a blue dress slips into my thoughts.

The pleasure builds, hollowing out my stomach, trapping my thoughts into a tourniquet as I thrust into my hand. Faster, harder, my mind melts into bare, basic instinct.

Hissing between my teeth, I glance up at Delilah's window, hating that I can't see her. If I could just see her...

Bending over, I yank the cock hard.

I wrench my eyes closed, determined to rip it off before it kills me.

Except...

Delilah in her dress slides back into my mind, her shapely legs, her soft brown hair, and the beat of her fluttering pulse when I stand too close to her.

Feeling death take hold, I arch sharply. Liquid sprays from the tip of my cock, squirting all over the scarecrow. A soul-deep tremble ripples through me as pleasure and unbearable, overwhelming bliss shreds me from within. My hips jerk, as my cock releases more spray, igniting another wave.

I hold in a roar as the explosion comes and goes, and when it's over, finally over, I pump my cock and do it all over again. Each release makes me looser, increasingly frustrated and incited by the need for something that I don't know how to get. I tug until my arm stiffens and my threads snap. Glaring down at my torrid cock, I know I've made a grave mistake.

I release my fist, shaking off the liquid caught on it. Liquid I ejaculated. I never expected to ejaculate. My body doesn't function like a human's; I don't bleed. Thick and opaque, my seed glints in the moonlight.

I taste it. It's the same taste that's been bothering me for days. Ever since Delilah and I kissed.

My nostrils flare at the thought of kissing her again, and my new cock bulges anew. Overcome, realizing thoughts of her no longer affect only me but also affect my cock, I shoot to my feet and pull up my jeans.

Cleaning my mess, I close up the barn. All of the house lights are off inside, and it's dark except for a small floodlight above the backdoor. Moths circle it as I pass by, entering the house's back door with ease. The smell of wet paper fills my nose as I take a look around. Furniture is gathered in the center of each room, covered in sheets. There are heaps of wallpaper everywhere.

She's making progress.

My jaw ticks.

Curious, I head to her room and nudge the door open. A beam of moonlight drifts from the window, casting the space within in deep silvery shadows.

Illuminated by them and tucked under her covers is Delilah. My lovely queen.

My hands clench as I approach the bed.

Her long hair is fanned out on the pillow. Partially on her side, she faces me, her eyes closed, her lips parted. A thin blue sheet is draped over her, covering her body from the torso down. Breathing evenly, her chest rises and falls in a steady rhythm.

I take in her form, tracing her curves. There has never been someone so intriguing as her, there has never been one who has taken my interest away from the crows.

I memorize every part of her. She exhales and shudders gently, shifting further onto her side. Curling her arms into her chest, she tucks her legs closer.

At first, I thought her a nuisance and then a plaything to toy with, to frighten. She has proven to be neither.

When she approaches me through the cornfield, the rustle of dried stalks heralding her, I quiver. I groan. The threads of my patches tighten.

She is not mine. Not yet.

But soon, she will be.

When I step back, my gaze catches on the image of an entwined couple on the cover of a book, one of many piled atop her bedside table. Curious about what brings the couple together, I shuffle through them. Pocketing the one on top, titled, *A Cowboy's Sweet Seduction*, I spare one more glance at my queen.

When I stumble across the yard, my limbs weary, the dark shadow of the Crow King appears.

"You've changed your body for her," he observes. "It is... curious."

He drifts away as quickly as he arrived, his words lingering behind him.

Collapsing several feet away from the platform, I drag my body under the structure and succumb to the fatigue.

Chapter Twenty-One
PREPARE

Delilah

Hauling the last of the wallpaper out of the house, I toss it in the dumpster. Tomorrow is pick-up day, and I want all of it gone. I never want to see floral wallpaper ever again. I'm tired of the mess. I miss walking around in socks and not worrying about what I might step on.

Trashing the paper also gives me an excuse to look for Jack. I thought we had patched things up, but now that it's evening and I haven't glimpsed him all day, I'm beginning to think I may have misunderstood where we stand.

Scanning the fields for him, I frown at the beautiful golden glow brightening the stalks. Crow's Rest has never looked so lovely, and I want to enjoy every second of it. I'm going to miss it when I'm back in the city and woken by loud neighbors or a car alarm.

He's not going to appear.

Disappointed, I head inside to clean up and make dinner. Tonight it's a peanut butter and jelly sandwich. I'm watching the sky change colors through the front dining room window when my phone rings.

Pulling it out of my pocket, I answer it with a sigh. "Hey, what's happening now?"

"No greeting? How rude," my brother says, acting scandalized.

I almost smile. Almost. "You're calling me in the middle of dinner." It's nice hearing his voice even if he drives me insane. The farm has been far too quiet lately.

"My bad. I just wanted to tell you the job posting was taken down, and I'm flying out there to visit on Friday."

"Haha. No, you're not. Aren't you coaching football camp?" I swallow the last bite and bring my plate to the sink. "Thanks for the update though."

"It ended last week. What did your boss say?"

I shrug and rinse off my plate. "Not much. Lacey, another trainer, is taking off six months for maternity leave. They need someone temporary to backfill. My job is still there."

"They must like you."

"They do."

"Surprising. You're the worst. Like, literally, a bitch queen of hell."

I chuckle. "And you're not? How is David by the way?"

"Last I heard, he was on a rock-climbing trip in Nevada."

My sister-in-law is presumably staying home with their kids. "Fun. Good for him."

"If you say so. I'm pretty sure he hasn't left the casinos yet. I don't know what Mom hates more, you off adventuring in the wilds of the Midwest alone or David scaling the red rocks and gambling. Neither are things she can brag about."

"Yeah, no kidding."

"She's not happy you won't answer her calls. You could do me a solid and pick up the phone next time. I hate being her only child here."

"I've got too much going on to justify being bogged down for three hours therapizing her. I told her the signal here sucks. You're just going to have to suck it up and keep her happy for a while longer."

"And yet... I always seem to get through. The signal can't be that bad."

I sigh. "Just don't tell her."

He sighs in return. "Whatever."

"I'll call her the next chance I get. The house is almost done, and that buyer I told you about, she's still interested. Hearing that will make Mom happy."

"Liar. I've seen pictures of Aunt Sylvie's farm—it should be wiped off the map. The place is a mess."

Insulted, I scrunch my face. "It's actually quite lovely."

"Look, I've got to go. I just got to the gym. I'll see you this weekend and you can show me yourself."

"Yeah right, and stop joking, this is my time, I don't need you to ruin it. Have fun lifting weights."

"I will."

"See ya."

"Chao."

He hangs up, and I begin to scroll through my texts. There are dozens from him and several from Mom, most left unanswered. Half of them are delayed because, despite managing short calls from my brother, the signal really is that bad.

The next morning, I start painting the interior, my eyes on the windows, always searching, always hoping he'll appear.

Two more days pass without a sign from Jack. I brave the edges of the fields, just enough to ensure they are properly watered. I call out his name and check the brook.

He's an adult. Older than me. He's fine.

I don't have his contact information or any way to reach him. I don't even know where he lives. If he quit and moved on, there's nothing I can do—but it bothers me, not knowing if he's safe.

After another day goes by, and there's still no sign of Jack, I absolve to head into town the next morning and speak with the county cops. Jack could be hurt out in the forest for all I know.

I'm not overreacting.

I'm not.

My stomach churns as I grab my keys, and throw open the front door. It's the crack of dawn as I head straight for my truck. A faint fog envelops the fields. Climbing in, I'm fumbling with the keys when I see something move in the corner of my eye.

Checking my rearview mirror, a figure emerges from the mists halfway down the driveway.

Jack.

He approaches with a bouquet of wildflowers. His eyes catch mine in the mirror, determined and unreadable, his face blank as we stare at each other. In his faded dark jeans and black shirt, he's also wearing a long black trench coat, the sight of which strikes me with déjà vu.

Stunned, and relieved, I watch as he strides over to me, and pops open the door to my truck.

He thrusts the flowers at me. "These are for you."

Having no choice but to take them, I look down at the black-eyed Susans and poppies in disbelief. I shove the flowers back at him and step out of the truck, slamming the door closed behind me.

"Where the hell have you been? I've been worried sick. For days, I heard nothing from you! I didn't know what to do. I searched for you! I was about to file a missing person's report.

How could you just leave without telling me? I have no way to reach you!"

He frowns at me.

I throw out my arms. "I was beginning to think you were hurt—dead maybe—stuck out there with a broken leg. How dare you show up out of the blue and think flowers will cut it. I should fire you!"

"Fire me?"

"Yes!" I shout, sending a crow fleeing. "Fire you! Pay you off and tell you to get the hell off my farm. I didn't get any fucking sleep last night, scared you might be out there in the forest and hurt!"

"You were worried about me?"

My nostrils flare. Worried? I'm furious.

But as I check him over, he looks fine, better than fine even. His clothes are clean and unwrinkled, and his hair is brushed out around his face and pulled back. With the flowers gripped in his hand, he looks like he put effort into his appearance.

I cross my arms. "Of course I was. Where have you been? And don't tell me it's not my business. I deserve to know."

He hands me back the flowers, and I gingerly accept, far from mollified.

"I did get hurt, and... I needed time to recover." He looks around, and his brow furrows. "Apparently I needed more time to recover than I realized."

I frown. "Are you okay?"

"I am now."

"You need to get a phone."

"That little device you carry around? I don't see the point."

"The point is that the next time you get hurt, you can call or text me to let me know." I scowl and head inside for something to put the flowers in.

Jack follows me. "I don't plan on getting hurt again."

"No one plans on getting hurt." Filling a tumbler cup with water, I plop the flowers in and place them in the kitchen window. "The last few days were awful. Don't you have anyone you'd call if you were hurt? There must be somebody." I face him. "Everyone has a phone these days."

"I haven't had any need for others before."

"What about your parents? Family?"

"I don't have any parents or family."

"No one?"

He shrugs and leans his hip on the counter. "No one."

"That's so sad..."

"If you say so."

His expression doesn't change. I can't imagine having no one else in the world. The farm is a great place to escape my family, but this was my choice.

I study him, always trying to figure him out. *He's like a lost puppy.* I shake my head. He's older than me by at least a decade; he's far from a lost puppy. He's more like a wolf, a wolf wearing a puppy costume.

I sigh and look at the flowers. "They're lovely, thank you."

"So you like them?"

"I do."

He smiles and threads his fingers through his hair.

I busy myself by pouring us both a cup of water. "Are you planning to work today?"

"I am..." His smile takes on a sly edge. "If I'm not fired."

"You're not fired. But I seriously was just on my way to the station. Don't put me in that position again." Part of me can't believe he's here, standing in front of me after all my fretting. I hand him a cup and sip from my own.

He sets it down on the counter. "I have no intention to, my queen," he says, his voice lowering enough to make my arms prickle.

Licking my lips, I shuffle away. "I'm not a queen."

"And yet calling you queen always gets a reaction out of you."

"It's a nice nickname. I can't help it."

I swallow, nervous. I can't tell if he's being flirty or ignorant. I don't want to be fooled.

"I like your smile." He raises his hand and swipes the back of his finger along my cheek. I stiffen as my stomach flutters. "I've learned a lot about myself these past few days—"

My phone rings, and I startle away from Jack's touch. I dig it out of my pocket and walk to the dining room to see who it is. Daniel's name appears.

After taking a long breath to deliberate, I let it go to voice-mail.

When I look up, Jack is behind me.

My backside bumps the table. "What are you—"

He kisses me.

I go rigid, standing prone as his lips press to mine, first firm and then soft and sweet, inviting me in. Warm and velvety, his mouth moves, deepening until my instincts take over and my lips move under his. One of his hands cups my nape as he draws me into him while also shuffling me onto the table. He nudges my legs open with his hips and presses his erection against me.

His very big, very stiff erection.

Overwhelmed, I grind, rubbing myself on him. I grab at his jacket, his shirt, clutching him everywhere.

"Jack." I moan his name.

He squeezes my nape and pulls back to look at me.

Staring at him, I reach for his zipper when my phone rings again.

Cursing, I shift away, grab it, and shut it off. When it's silent, I turn back, meeting his hungry gaze.

This is happening. I wipe my mouth with the back of my hand.

He's tense, his hands clenched, his body practically shaking. "I want you," he whispers, his voice rough.

"I want you too," I say so quietly I barely hear my own words.

He straightens as a wicked, eager look flickers across his face. "It's settled then."

"What's settled?"

"We're partners now, you and I. There will be no one else from now on. Tonight I will make you dinner, and afterward, my queen, you'll take my cock."

My mouth drops. "What?"

With one last scan of my face, his haughty eyes taking me in from head to toe, he bows his head like he's some gentleman. "Prepare yourself."

And with that, he strides out, leaving me speechless.

CHAPTER TWENTY-TWO

YOU

DELILAH

I continue painting while Jack trucks vegetables in from the garden. He's in and out, bringing his collection to the kitchen counter.

Each time he passes me in the hallway, his gaze devours me.

It's been a long day as I struggle to focus on anything besides cock. His cock. I'm mentally exhausted by the time I paint a second coat along the trim. Silent and predatory, his words are branded in my head.

Prepare yourself.
You'll take my cock.
Prepare yourself.

No matter how many times I repeat them, they never fail to make me freeze as my throat tightens with all the ways I could prepare for him. Losing focus, my hand slips, and I get paint all over the trim.

At that moment, Jack pushes open the front door with a bushel of greens in his arms. He looks at me on my knees and goes rigid. My gaze drops to the erection he's been suffering with all day.

As he walks away, I wonder how I've failed to notice his package until now. Because it's big and noticeable. It's hard to miss. How was I that ignorant? That's the true mystery here. I've checked him out countless times.

Grabbing a towel, I wipe the paint off the trim and sit back on my heels. Hearing the sink running, I stand and take a peek into the kitchen to see what he's up to.

He lifts a giant purple eggplant and inspects it before wiping it dry and setting it on the counter with several others.

He's cleaning vegetables.

"The plates are in the cabinet to your left," I say.

He looks over his shoulder, first at me and then at where I'm pointing. Drying his hands, he opens the cabinet.

"Use whatever you need," I add.

He nods and pulls out a couple of plates. Jack acting domestic is not something I've ever envisioned. Domestic or romantic.

He's more like a wild animal than the house-husband type.

I head to the hallway to clean up, and by the time I'm done with my mess, Jack is still at the sink. Deciding not to bother him, I head upstairs to shower, slowly walking past the kitchen one last time.

Jack is rummaging through the cabinets and drawers, pulling out random bowls and utensils.

He's definitely a wild animal.

"I know you're watching me, Delilah."

I fumble at his voice then curse. "You can't be certain of that."

"I can. I know everything that is happening on this farm, even if I can't see it." He faces me and crosses his arms.

"Uh-huh, yeah. Right."

A blush rises to my cheeks as I slink away.

I spend the next few hours doing exactly what he said: preparing. But the closer it gets to evening, the more my nerves fray. It's been years since I last slept with anyone or anyone's seen me naked. As much as I like to fantasize I'm some sex goddess, I couldn't be further from it.

I opt to wear my untorn jeans and one of my nicer shirts. Besides my ruined blue dress, I have nothing cute to wear, not even underwear. All my undergarments are white and bland, so I go for the only matching set I have.

I tiptoe downstairs and enter the dining room, pausing on the threshold. Fruits and vegetables are laid out on plates across the table in the design of a flower, with the brightest colored fruits as the petals, and the greens as the stem and leaves. Amongst them are real flowers, filling out the shape, and interspersed candles, their wicks already lit. Only two chairs remain, facing one another at the center, and placed before them are empty plates, glasses of water, and folded napkins.

At the head of the table is the bouquet Jack gave me this morning.

"This is..." I hesitate, approaching the setup, surprised at the length he's gone through to make this evening romantic. "It's like a fairy garden. It's beautiful."

He turns at my voice, his eyes ablaze. "There are and will be no faeries here."

I laugh at his tone when I meet his gaze. "Of course not."

"They are evil, malicious creatures, making false promises."

"Okay."

"If you ever encounter one, run."

"Jack! I was joking."

He gifts me a look that says he doesn't care, and I know he's serious.

"Fine." I sigh. "If I ever see a fairy, I'll run."

"Good."

"The table is beautiful," I repeat.

He scans me over like he's weighing whether or not I'm telling the truth. "I'm glad it pleases you."

"Is this all from the garden?"

With a bowl of glistening blackberries in his hand, he joins me. "Some of the flowers are from around the house."

"I love it. I'm not very creative. I never would have thought of using them."

His gaze sharpens on me. Setting down the blackberries, he goes to the chair farthest away and tugs it out. "Sit."

Acutely aware his erection is as blunt as ever, I undertake the long journey across the room toward him. I sit as I'm told, and he pushes me in until I'm positioned comfortably. Taking hold of my plate, he fills it with the choicest pieces.

I watch in silence as he works, creating a plate that looks more like a piece of art than a meal. He drizzles honey onto the berries as the finale before placing it in front of me.

He steps back as I look down at the vibrant, fresh colors. "I can't believe this all came from the garden." I can't believe Jack made me a beautiful plate of food.

"The land can grow anything you want. You just need to seed it."

I scoop up a berry with my spoon. "I like that."

"It's true."

We fall into silence as he heads to the other side of the table and sits down. He cups his hands under his chin and leans on them, his eyes devouring me like they've done all day.

All the while, his plate remains empty. "You're not eating?"

"Does it bother you that I'm not?"

"Yes. I don't want to eat alone."

He picks up a strawberry and places it in his mouth, chewing with oversized motions. His eyes widen into orbs, and his jaw slows to a crawl.

I lower my spoon. "Are you okay?"

A myriad of emotions has streaked across his face by the time he swallows, concluding in awe. "That was…" He looks down at the plate of strawberries before him. "A strawberry."

I can't help laughing. "What else would it be?" Reaching across the table, I pick one up and eat it. "Yep, strawberry."

His brows furrow as he studies the rest of the display on the table. "The taste is incredible."

"You should eat more of them then. I never see you eat. You're welcome to use the refrigerator to store your lunch. I should've said that months ago, sorry."

His gaze flicks back to me. "I don't want to eat more. What I want is to put my cock inside you."

My spoon drops as my lips part and the romantic pretense of dinner slips away. My stomach tightens as heat pools between my legs, and I fold my hands into my lap, trying to form a reply.

He stands and walks slowly back around the table.

Jack's not a puppy, nor a wolf.

He's a jackal.

He's not going to be some mere summer fling. He's going to destroy me.

CHAPTER TWENTY-THREE

EAT OR BE EATEN

DELILAH

He stops at my side and pets my hair, brushing it behind my ear.

At his touch, my brain stutters. "What happened to you?" I whisper, wondering if something more happened while he was gone.

He kneels, cups my knees, and pushes my legs apart. "What do you mean? I want to be closer to you." Jack runs his hands up my thighs and then takes mine into his own, pulling me up with him. "I told you that."

Before I can respond, he slams his mouth to mine. Frantically his lips move, his tongue demanding entry, the kiss entirely different from our first. I moan under the onslaught and clutch onto him. He guides me away from the table and toward the stairs where I lean against the wall and wrap my hand around his neck. Rubbing his erection against me, I grind into him.

I gasp, digging my nails into his shoulders. He traps me against him, standing tall to break the kiss, and clutches me into his arms. He carries me the rest of the way upstairs. I swallow the instinct to protest and demand he take me right here.

As he holds me close, I breathe him in, soap and clean summer air filling my nose.

He lays me down on my bed and crawls on top of me, burying his face into my neck. Exhaling against my skin, he licks my throat.

I hear my shirt rip, his hands twisting the fabric. Next, he tugs at my bra. Straddling me, he sits up and looks down now that I'm naked from the waist up.

His eyes flash yellow.

I frown as he reaches down his pants and pulls out his cock.

My lips part.

It's thick, his girth bulging like it's swollen. My stomach hollows out as he cups it, running his palm along the rounded bottom, traveling it along his slightly tapered tip. He finishes by squeezing it.

My legs close. "Oh no."

Oh my god. I'm not woman enough for him. This was a mistake.

He doesn't realize my horror as he leans over me and yanks off my pants.

"Jack!"

He drops my jeans on the ground and looks up. "What?"

"You are way out of my league, with—with—" I pull my legs under me and point at the club hanging heavily between his thighs. "That."

"Don't worry. This was mentioned in the book. It will fit."

"Book? What book?"

"The cowboy one."

"What?" I glance at the stack of cowboy romances next to my bed.

Without answering, he grabs my legs out from under me and thrusts my knees apart, climbing onto the bed between them.

"Jack!"

He responds by pushing me flat and pinning my legs to my chest. "All I have to do is make you really wet and stretch you with my fingers. With enough coaxing and enough work, you'll be able to accommodate all of me."

"Wait, did you learn about sex from the cowboy book?"

He stills. "Is that a problem?"

"I... Well, maybe not."

He grins, and grabbing my underwear, he rips them when they catch on my knees. Squirming my hips, I don't know if I'm more aroused or terrified by his confidence.

Then, with his hands still holding my legs to my chest, and completely open to him, he presses his lips to my clenching sex.

I hitch—fear, excitement, and arousal surging with a rush of adrenaline. Flattening his tongue to my core, he licks up to my clit. My body buckles in response.

"I knew you would taste good."

I slump back and moan, giving in as Jack licks me from core to clit like my pussy is a lollipop—like if he licks me enough, he can consume me.

"Please," I beg, reaching down to grab his head and hold it between my legs. His cock scares me, but my courage grows with each lash of his tongue.

A knocking noise comes from downstairs.

I ignore it, but Jack hesitates, and when it remains quiet, he presses his finger into me.

I cry out as he pushes against the sensitive wall inside me, shocked to be penetrated and probed. Hips shaking, I adjust to his finger digging into my g-spot. He starts to add another when the knocking sounds again.

Jack's fingers stall.

I go tense, peering past him and into the hallway. "Someone's here."

"Who?" he growls, like murder is on his mind as he pulls his fingers out of me.

I glance at them and whimper my disappointment. "I don't know."

The knocking sounds again, harder, more urgent this time.

Jack climbs off me, and I join him, throwing on the first clothes I can find. He stays near, tugging up his jeans. When I turn to leave, there's a scowl on his face and a... glow in his eyes.

Just a trick of the light.

The thumping sounds again, followed by a yell. Startled, I dart past him.

At the front door, I check the peephole and groan, yanking it open.

Daniel.

I've never seen him more pissed.

"I can't fucking believe you!" he shouts, barging into my house. "I called you fifty fucking times! I left voicemails and texts. The least you could have done is answer, for fuck's sake!"

"I can't believe you came." I chase after him. "I told you not to come!"

He drops his duffle and rounds on me. "Well, I didn't listen, did I? And apparently, neither did you."

"Why are you here?"

"To check up on my baby sister, why else? I wanted to make sure you were okay."

Right. "I don't believe you for a second."

He rolls his eyes. "Does it matter? Because I'm here now, and that's not going to change."

My nostrils flare. "How dare you." I've never been so mad, and he's the only one I moderately get along with in my family.

What's worse, the heat in my face isn't because of him being here, it's because I still feel Jack's finger petting me, pressing inside me, readying me for his cock. I'm angry that, of all the times Daniel could have dropped in, it had to be right now.

Jack grabs my wrist and turns me to face him. "Delilah? Should I get rid of him?"

Daniel takes a step toward us. "Who's he?"

Suddenly nervous and moving between them, I block their path to one another. "He's a... He's someone who's working on the farm with me. Daniel, I want you to leave, please. It's time for you to go."

He ignores me and glowers at Jack, but then upon seeing the table, the candles, and the ornate display of food, his face turns red.

Sensing what's about to happen and tugging my arm out of Jack's grip, I grab my brother's duffle and throw it at him. "Get out, Daniel. You shouldn't have come. We can talk tomorrow when you calm down. Get a motel room."

"Who is he, Delilah?" He ignores me and looks at Jack again.

"He's none of your business. Please go."

I don't want to make my brother more upset than he already is.

"Of course it's my business if some man is trying to get with you."

"No, it's not. And I know you mean well, but—"

Daniel shoves his duffle into my arms and pushes me aside. He gets up in Jack's face. "Who the fuck do you think you are trying to fuck my sister?"

Jack's on top of him in the next instant. He pins my brother to the floor and punches him in the face.

I drop the duffle with a shout.

Recovering from the attack, my brother throws Jack off. Rolling onto his feet, Jack grabs Daniel's shirt collar and throws him into the wall.

"Stop!"

Pressing his arm against Daniel's throat, Jack stops Daniel before he can throw another punch.

"She said get out."

Daniel growls. "Fuck you."

"Stop it! Now, both of you!" I crowd between them and pull Jack's arm from my brother's throat. Stepping back, he shakes out his hand. I face Daniel. "Damn the both of you! Are you okay?"

My brother wipes his nose on his sleeve and scowls at me, getting blood everywhere. "If you want me to leave, fine. But don't expect me to stand up for you anymore."

He shoves past me again and snatches his bag, spitting blood onto the floor. Storming out the door, I chase after him. "Daniel, you're hurt."

He gets into his car and slams the door in my face. Starting up his vehicle, he gives me the finger as he drives away.

When I can't hear his car anymore, I draw my fists to my face and scream.

Hundreds of crows startle out of the fields and soar into the night. Shocked, I watch as they flee into the forest, leaving me alone with Jack who waits for me at the doorway. Exhaling, I face him.

Furious, his jaw ticks.

"I'm sorry," I say.

"Who was that?"

"Daniel. My brother."

"Your... brother?"

"Yeah, one of two, I'm afraid. Jack, if you want to leave..." Of course he'd want to leave. Who wants to stay after something like that? Being forced into a fight with a man who's been abusing steroids for years?

Suddenly exhausted, my shoulders sag, and I shuffle past him and into the foyer. Behind me, I hear him close and lock the door.

"Look, about earlier..." I shudder from the memory of his tongue between my legs, his fingers inside me. "I liked what we were doing." I try not to stare at his chest or peek at his groin. "But after what just happened…"

"You're scared."

"I'm shaken."

He nods, and I relax.

He tugs me into his arms and rests his chin on my head. "No one is allowed to scare you except me."

Any confusion over his words is swept away when, for the second time that evening, he lifts me into his arms and carries me to my room.

"You can stay if you want," I whisper when he's about to put me down on the bed.

He cocks his head, and I can't tell what he's thinking. Shifting back and grabbing the covers, I slide my legs under and then lift the corner, inviting him to slide his legs under too.

Slowly he climbs into the bed beside me and rests his head on the pillow.

I shuffle onto my side to face him. "Thank you for staying."

"Of course, my queen."

I can't help the small smile that creeps across my lips. Sleep finally comes as I'm resting against his chest wondering where his heartbeat is.

Chapter Twenty-Four
UNRAVELED

DELILAH

My toes brush against Jack's leg, and my gaze shifts to him. Sleeping beside me, he's so deep in his dreams that his body is stiff.

Determined to make the most of the morning, I slip out of bed, throw on some clothes, and head downstairs. The flowers he brought are still the centerpiece of the dining table, surrounded by remnants from the dinner, and I pause, leaning in to appreciate his handiwork for another moment.

Heading to the back barn, I unlock it and shove open the doors, planning to clear the craft table and move it out front.

I want to surprise Jack and serve him breakfast in the garden, so I can show him how badly I want to start over.

That, even if Daniel is my brother, he doesn't have to worry about him.

After setting the table up by the garden, I head back to the barn for the chairs, catching sight of the scarecrow from the other day. I pause when I realize that the cock Jack had so carefully attached to it is gone. He must have changed his mind.

I find the foldout chairs stacked behind it and out of reach. I'm moving the scarecrow aside when my grip slips and my arm bumps something.

Jack's scythe clatters to the floor.

I bend over to pick it up, finding there's an engraving at the top. Curious, I lift the scythe closer to read it.

Hollowstalk is etched in the wood.

I read it a dozen more times.

This is Hollowstalk's scythe?

I tossed it in town with the rest of him...

My palms grow clammy. Why is Jack using a scythe I tossed? Peering up at my bedroom window, my stomach clamps knowing he's right on the other side, lying in my bed.

He showed up the morning after I tossed Hollowstalk out. *Jack's last name is* Hollow.

He knows things about the farm he shouldn't.

It's not a coincidence. It never was.

Taking the scythe with me, I change my plans about breakfast and head for Hollowstalk's platform. If Jack has the scythe, what other obscure interest might he have in the old scarecrow?

When I reach the old platform, I pause to look around. I haven't been here since midsummer's night, and it's different surrounded by fully grown stalks. I clamber up the perch, finding it completely unremarkable. The fields span out all around me, idly swaying in the breeze. Looking down, I scan the wood slats at my feet.

There's something there.

I jump off the platform, put the scythe aside, and get on my knees to look.

There's a neat stack of clothes that I recognize as Jack's. I pull out several more garments and a rugged pair of black pants that are folded strangely. When I tug them loose, two books tumble from the folds.

The anatomy and physiology book Jack was reading during the storm and a romance from my aunt's collection.

The cowboy book...

I stare from one cover to the other, the graphic of a human skeleton at complete odds with the bare-chested man, his hand around a woman's back, her dress slipping off the shoulder to expose her busty cleavage.

Another item falls out.

A crow's skull with a leather throng strung through its eye sockets.

I drop the necklace. *It's the one he wore.*

When I raise my gaze, it lands on Redeyes. He stares down at me from the top of the scarecrow's post.

He caws and points his beak toward the house. Frowning up at him, I wonder if he's trying to tell me something. It wouldn't be the strangest thing to have occurred...

Grabbing the scythe and the skull necklace, I stand as anger and nervousness ripple through me. I clutch Hollowstalk's items harder, finally having had enough of it all. Straightening, I turn full circle deciding what I should do.

CHAPTER TWENTY-FIVE

TO LAY BARE THE TRUTH

I'm relaxed despite my cock remaining stiff all night, eager to nudge between Delilah's legs, sink inside her, and pleasure her with my thrusts.

Reaching for her, my hand slides across cold sheets. When I open my eyes, I'm greeted by empty, rumpled bedding.

I sit upright, shove the blankets off, and jolt out of bed, alarmed she could have gotten away without me noticing, that the addition of my cock is compromising me. Pacing through the empty living room, den, kitchen, and dining room, I head for the front door.

Yanking it open, I stop short. At the bottom of the porch steps, Delilah holds my scythe in one hand while the other has my necklace dangling from its grip. Sweat glistens across her chest, her face prettily flushed. The sight of her clutching my scythe makes my cock tighten all over again as I picture her hand wrapped around something else that's mine...

When she sees me, she takes a step back, fear evident in the way she shies away from me. She searches my face as her brows form a deep crease between her eyes. "Why do you have these things?" Her tone is flat and accusatory.

I glance between her and my necklace, spying the Crow King's emissary behind her, watching us from the rooftop of the garden shed. He flaps his wings, clearly entertained.

My gaze slides back to Delilah as a scowl forms on my lips. I take in her ashen skin, not liking it one bit.

"I found them," I lie. She doesn't want the truth—even if she thinks she does, even if she has the evidence in her hands, she doesn't want to know about this.

"I found your scythe in the barn, or should I say Hollowstalk's scythe. Then the anatomy book under the platform, the cowboy romance too. Your clothes were there. And also... this." She looks down at the skull. "I know this is Hollowstalk's. He was wearing it when I dumped him."

I take a step forward. "I never meant to hurt you."

She shuffles back. "Why is this stuff here? Are you trying to fuck with my head? Is that it? Jack—if that is your name—tell me or I'm calling the police. Because you've messed with it alright. I don't know what to think anymore!"

"Nothing I say will be easy for you to hear."

Her face scrunches with suspicion. "How can I trust anything you say? It's about the Crow King, isn't it? Are you part of some local cult and conned your way into my life?"

I take another step forward, determined to stop her if she tries to get into her vehicle. "Everything I've told you has been the truth."

"Crow Kings aren't real!"

"The evidence is in your hands."

"What, an old scarecrow's scythe and his macabre necklace are proof of the supernatural? That doesn't make any sense!"

"They're not some old scarecrow's. Those items are mine and always have been," I snap.

"How could they possibly be yours?"

"I've been here since the beginning."

She shifts my scythe like a shield against me.

"You don't have to be afraid of me or of what I am. I would never hurt you." The words taste like dirt on my tongue.

"You have five minutes. Convince me that you're telling me the truth or leave. Because if you don't, I'm calling the police."

I thread my fingers through my hair. "Delilah, this farm is all I've ever had. I have lived here since the beginning."

She stares at me. "You have got to be kidding me if you think any of that is going to help me believe you. The farm was built nearly two centuries ago! You're trying to tell me you've been here all that time? That's impossible."

"Yes, I've been here since the first owner, Winifred Meriweather and then I aided Lydia, her daughter-in-law. When Lydia mistakenly put her trust in the Comings, their daughter Mary set things back to right. Mary was followed by the Shorewoods. Then there was Ivar and your aunt. Now you, Delilah Mackay, are the seventh to take ownership of this land."

Her eyes dart as I name each of her predecessors. "What does that make you then?"

"Winifred crafted me and gave me consciousness."

She blinks at me.

"In exchange, I care for the crops, guarding them from the crows and also, if necessary, am a mediator between them and the pactholder."

Her gaze flicks to the scythe. "None of this explains why you have the scythe and necklace or why your clothes are out there!" She points the scythe at the field behind her.

My fingers twitch as her expression grows more incredulous. "What I'm trying to say is... I *am* Hollowstalk."

She goes still, her brow furrowing. She lowers my weapon.

"Do you want me to prove it?" I ask.

She studies me, her eyes squinting. "Yes."

I reach out my hand. "Give me the scythe."

She searches my face once more before glancing at my outstretched hand, her grip tightening on its shaft.

"I will never hurt you," I whisper. "I am here to help, not hurt."

Slowly, her face softens and her grip loosens. She tilts the scythe forward, and I grab the top of the pole before it wobbles. She releases it as I tug it from her hands, and our eyes lock.

She wants to trust me. She's willing to try.

I watch her face as I lower the blade of my scythe, wrap my hand around it, and yank.

Hay and straw spring from the slash across my palm. Delilah jerks but doesn't protest. Putting the scythe aside, I show her my hand, palm side up.

Concern crosses her face as she glances back at me.

"Look," I order, outstretching my fingers.

Curiosity replaces her concern, and she leans forward, cups my hand, and stares.

As she runs her finger along the seams of the cut, the edges of my skin roughen, more akin to cloth. She stares, her expression forming one of awe.

"Can I... touch you—explore further?" she asks, suddenly shy yet interested. "I was a trainer back home—I helped people with their bodies."

"Go ahead."

She runs her hands across my arm, shoulders, back, and even my chest, testing and probing my body. Heat spreads through me, following wherever her fingertips lead before pouring into my cock. It stiffens, returning to its persistently torturous ache.

"Do you feel pain?" she asks.

"I'm not sure. There are good sensations and... uncomfortable ones. I would take the bad over feeling nothing at all."

My jaw clenches in the struggle to keep my erection down.

"Do you bleed?"

"No."

She circles me. "And you don't eat."

"Except strawberries."

The corner of her lips twitch. "You feel human. You're warm..." Her voice lowers. "How is that possible?"

"The warmth began in June. It happened after the windmill. When I decided to start watching you closer."

The furrow in her brow returns. "I haven't been paranoid then. You *have* been watching me?"

"All the time. Every moment of every day, I watch you. When I am forced away, a hunger grows within me until you are back within my sight. It's torturous, being away from you."

Her lips part, and her hands drop from my body. She looks away like she's embarrassed or she's considering something. Having no idea what, I wish I could crawl into her head and read her thoughts.

Then suddenly, she leans in and presses her ear to my chest.

My hands uncurl, confused by her actions, and my arms loosen to embrace her. Does she wish for me to hold her? To warm her?

Before I can pull her close, she draws away. "No heartbeat."

"No heart."

Surprise and sadness streak across her expression. "I don't believe it. You need a heart."

"No, I don't. Let me show you." Retrieving my scythe, I point the tip toward my chest. "Don't be frightened." Tipping the blade closer, I dig it into my chest, ripping at the skin-turned-fabric. I hold her gaze, reassuring her that I'm not going to suddenly unravel, and push my fingers into me until my entire fist is inside. Pulling it out, I show her a fistful of my stuffing.

I take her palm and press my insides into it. "I'm not human. I'm nothing like you. What you see before you, these human features, they're not what I really am. What I *am* is Hollow-stalk."

Chapter Twenty-Six

It's All in the Stuffing

Delilah's face whitens. The passing seconds are slow as I wait for her to respond. Finally, she looks down at her hand.

Eyes wide, she leans in to examine the stuffing and sort through it.

She pauses then gives me back the clump. Her silence frustrates me as she stares while I press it back into me. I don't know what I'll do if she sends me away now, or worse, leaves and doesn't return. The thought of losing her...

"Jack..." she whispers. "I believe you."

"Will you stay?"

"Stay?"

"Stay? At the farm?"

Delilah looks around like she's suddenly remembering where she is. "I don't know. I have questions."

"Ask them," I demand, picking up my scythe and putting distance between us, annoyed that she doesn't know the answer outright.

She eyes me warily, her brown eyes thoughtful. "You scared me that night I saw you outside my window. I was terrified. You... Oh my god, you broke my air unit, didn't you?"

"You threw me in the trash." My jaw ticks.

"But I put you in a dumpster miles from here. How did you know where to go?"

"Winifred's magic drew me back."

Her brow furrows at the mention of Winifred. "Why not come to me as Jack earlier? Why... wait?"

"Until you failed to seed the land, I never had a reason to move, to do more than watch and become what I am now. I had no reason to try, and so I never did." Fisting my scythe, frustrated with the omission, I turn away and walk toward the field.

"Where are you going?" she calls out as I storm across the yard.

"To gather my things."

I hear her give chase. "Why? Why me?"

My hands clench and unclench again, trying not to turn on her and show her why. "You needed help."

"Oh... Well, You did a good job fooling me into thinking that you were human..."

"You knew nothing about this place and had no reason to expect anything."

"I guess this explains some of the bizarre things you say."

Coming upon the platform, I grab a shirt and pull it on to stop Delilah's eyes from roaming over the tear in my chest. I want her to see me as human, and not the monstrous thing I am beneath.

I turn on her. "Before, I could see most everything on this land, instinctually knowing what was happening. I always knew if any thieves were slinking near the corn, and wherever the crows targeted, I could be there like a shadow to scare them off."

She looks down and then hands me something. My necklace is tucked in her palm. "You should have this back."

My nostrils flare. "Keep it."

She hesitates but then slowly draws her hand away. She hugs herself and steps toward the house. "I need coffee. Can we talk after?"

Watching her carefully, I nod.

Struggling to understand her reactions, I follow her into the house, closing the front door behind me, relieved that she's allowing me inside. With her gaze avoiding mine, she scurries past the dining table where last night's creation remains mostly untouched.

I lean against the counter and wait as she preps her drink.

The coffee machine beeps, and Delilah's chest expands with her long breath. "I don't want you to be telling the truth. Living is easier when there's a justification for everything, but after what you've shown me... I don't know if I'm numb or just coming to terms." She rubs her forehead. "What is the Crow King anyhow?"

I cross my arms and glance out the window for his emissary. "He's the god of corvids—crows, ravens, and jays. He is the oldest of them and is their king."

"Right. Okay. So he's a... bird?"

I hesitate. "He takes various forms, but yes, he's a bird."

"So what happens if the pact fails? Do I get pecked at again? Spanked?"

I frown, glancing at her backside, flexing my hands. "It's happened once before with the Comings. They sold the entirety of the crop to pay off their debts."

"They vanished, right? At Halloween?"

"When the tribute was due and they had none, they were taken by the Crow King and transformed into crows."

Her face pales. "What happened next?"

"Their daughter, Mary, negotiated with the Crow King for the pact to continue."

"Negotiated?"

"She offered the entirety of her first harvest for the pact to continue—ensuring she would be hungry herself the following winter—and the Crow King agreed." When she glances out the window, I follow her gaze. Outside, the emissary watches us, surrounded by a growing flock of birds. They caw, greeting the morning as the last of the fog evaporates.

"What is that bird? The one I call Redeyes," she asks after a moment.

"He's an emissary. He leads the flock."

"He doesn't like me very much."

"He's worried the flock will go hungry this winter."

"I see." She grows silent again, watching the crows, and when she finally turns to face me, her gaze lands on my face before dropping to my hand. "Do you need stitches or something for that?"

I shift away from the counter and show her my hand when she approaches me. "I'll be fine. I can sew my tears closed."

She sets her coffee mug down. "You did it to make your point. You did it for me. Let me help." She grabs a chair from the table and spins it toward me. "Sit."

She leaves, and I eye the chair in her wake. Yearning for her touch, deciding that she can't make my tears worse, I sit and wait.

"Will this work?" She walks into the dining room with a needle and yarn. "I got it from the supplies in the barn."

It's the same stuff I used for my cock. I give her a sharp nod.

Delilah kneels on the floor, takes my hand, peels open my fingers, and pinches the fabric closed. "I'll make a line here?" she asks. "And for the record, I don't know how you were going to sew your own hand without my help."

At the sight of her kneeling before me, my teeth grind. "I would have figured it out."

She sews me closed in silence, leaving behind a thin scar that will shortly fade. Tying off the string, she smooths her thumbs over the crease.

She clears her throat and looks up at me. "Should I do your chest next?"

I don't want her to stop so I take off my shirt in response.

She stands, forced to shuffle between my spread legs to get close enough. Her cheeks turn a bright red as she stitches me closed. When she's done, she ties off the thread and moves away. The resulting stitches cover my nonexistent heart with a thicker scar that will take longer to fade.

"Thank you."

"It's the least I can do."

I sit forward. "So, what happens now?"

Her gaze flicks to mine. "I don't know." She heads to the counter and picks up her coffee.

I throw on my shirt and follow her.

She spins and puts up her hand like she's trying to ward me off. "Don't." She inhales. "Please."

With a frown, I pause.

"I think..." She swallows and lowers her hand. "I need time to process."

Wishing I knew what to say to stay with her, I head for the door.

She grabs my arm. "Hollowstalk." Her face softens when I look back at her. "You really did terrify me that night but... I forgive you. And you might not think you have a heart, but I know you do. You don't have to be human to have a heart."

Leaving me frozen in her foyer, she disappears upstairs and out of sight. I walk outside, head into the stalks, and face the house, already hungry for my next glimpse.

CHAPTER TWENTY-SEVEN

UNSEWN AND UNDONE

DELILAH

Jack is Hollowstalk, a scarecrow. And I believe him.

How could I not, after seeing his body cut open and handling his insides. I myself stitched his wounds closed.

I finished painting yesterday and am unsure what to do next. I wander the house and barns, seizing upon whatever mindless task crosses my path. I've untangled a knot of extension cables, washed the sunroom windows, and pressure-washed the outside of the shed because I've decided it needs a new coat of paint as well.

Through every chore, Jack gives me a wide berth. Somewhere, amongst the mundane tasks, I let any remaining skepticism I had go. It's been easier to adjust without him. I can take my time. There's nothing else to distract me... like the fact that we almost had sex and that his... tongue and fingers have explored my pussy.

A scarecrow's fingers and tongue...

Every time I imagine *Hollowstalk* kissing me, touching me the way Jack had, my throat tightens, and my head clouds with confusion.

And this arousal, while inconvenient, is only the start of my problems.

I'm beholden to a god.

Finding a suitable buyer for the farm has become much more complicated. No wonder Sylvie left things to me, and only me, rather than dividing her assets. No one else in the family would have come out here. They would have sold everything and never thought about it again.

At least until a crow god showed up for its corn.

Searching for my next distraction, I eye the empty garden beds. The day of his dinner, Jack cleared it out, opening space for new plants. I've found seeds for winter vegetables in the shed: carrots, kale, and beans.

As I leave the house, I look up to see Jack watching me, his leather gloves in hand by the back barn.

"Jack," I call out in a moment of courage. "Can you help me?"

He strides over, his dark eyes piercing mine. His trousers bulge, concealing his enormous package. It's obvious he isn't human now that he's not trying to hide it anymore.

With him illuminated by the midday sun, the fluttering in my belly grows. He's darker somehow, wilder, eerie even.

What if his desire is a ruse?

"What do you need?" He checks me over, blatant in his perusal.

My mouth goes dry. "I want... I want to plant seeds."

Shadows creep across his face, and I catch a glimpse of Hollowstalk. It's in the shape of his nose, the texture of his hair, and the yellow glint of his eyes.

He smiles, and the delusion fades away. All I see is Jack, a man I've come to trust, not a scarecrow.

"First we will prepare the soil with compost," he rasps, moving away to push the garden's wheelbarrow to the compost pile.

He rakes the soil, bringing forth a section from the bottom that has completely devolved into thick dirt. The pile radiates warmth, scented like soil. With gloved hands, he pushes it into a bucket and empties that into the wheelbarrow. Mimicking him, I follow suit.

Except for some innocuous questions, I remain silent as he explains to me what he does as he does it before letting me take over. After a time, any strangeness between us fades. When the wheelbarrow is full, Jack combs over the entirety of the pile, mixing it up and then watering it down.

"It's hard to believe we made this from waste," I say.

"That's the power of earth, the cycle of change."

When he carries the hose to the garden, I push the wheelbarrow behind him.

Jack grabs two trowels from the shed. "Now we mix in the compost."

We comb through the soil, finding clumps and breaking them apart. Adding water, we ensure the soil is moist. We add compost, turning it over until it is thoroughly mixed.

I help him pat the soil flat, and when my fingers land on his, our gloves coming between us, I don't shift them away. I press my hand down.

He flips his palm over, weaving his fingers through mine, and I still don't shy away, entwining my hand with his. Despite the gloves, his grip is tight.

There's even a stray piece of straw sticking out from the side of his neck.

I reach for it, following down its length until I find the point where it secures to his nape, right under his hairline.

He holds my gaze.

I draw my hand away.

Jack looks away first and some of the strain in my shoulders releases. At least until I glance over his constant erection and suck in a breath.

"Now that the soil is tilled and damp, we plant," he says, his voice low.

He uses his trowel to form a low trench in the soil. When he's done, he opens an envelope of carrot seeds. Taking my hand, he flips it palm side up and pours the seeds into it. They're small brown things that could be easily dismissed.

"Plant them," he directs me.

I do as he says, scattering them in the trough while he sweeps the displaced soil into place.

Afterward, Jack leans down until his lips are inches above the soil. He breathes upon one of the rows, waits a moment, and does it again.

A sliver of green peeks through the dirt. Another one joins it. And before my eyes, I watch as the seeds we planted germinate.

"How—"

Jack sits upright. "Winifred's magic. It remains within me, enabling me to care for this farm." He smiles until scar lines form at the corners of his lips becoming stitches. The face of a scarecrow. I gape, and he frowns at me, returning his features to before. "It tires me, working the earth in this way, and it becomes difficult to maintain my appearance. I've hidden it before, but now, I think you should know what's possible."

I look down at the seedlings, wondering what else he can do—what else can be *done*. "That's amazing..." People spend their entire lives searching for what Jack just showed me, praying that there's magic out there somewhere. And here it is, in front of me.

But the sight bothers me in a way that has nothing to do with Jack or magic.

"My brother uses steroids," I blurt out when another group of seedlings sprout.

Jack pauses and looks at me.

"Steroids accelerate growth in humans, enhancing muscle development with nasty side effects. My brother started taking them in college. He can get... angry."

"And that makes him dangerous?"

"No, but he can be... *a lot*. We used to be close, but the steroids changed him. I miss who he used to be."

Jack studies me, and I'm reminded of how little he knows about things outside Crow's Rest.

"My family is complicated," I offer with a shrug. "Most are. Sorry I changed the subject..."

"I've watched the families that have lived here. They're all I know of them."

My heart aches at his words. I can't imagine watching the world go by without being part of it.

He glances at the plants. "I didn't mean to remind you of something painful."

"No, it's not that. My mind wandered. He went home, by the way. We met up for coffee and I told him to leave," I add just in case he's curious.

"I noticed he hasn't returned."

My lips purse. "Because you've been watching me."

He doesn't even hesitate. "Was I supposed to stop?"

Swallowing, hoping I can keep my cheeks from heating, I turn my attention to the completed rows. "What's next?"

Jack sits back on his heels and strips off his gloves. "Are you staying?" he asks, leveling with me.

Avoiding his question, I sigh and look around. "I wish I had known—believed sooner—I don't want the crows to go hungry on my account or you to..." I trail off because not knowing what would happen to him has been on my mind.

"To fade?"

"Is that what would happen if the pact was broken?"

His eyes narrow. "Don't worry about me. I have been around for a long time. I plan to be around for a long time to come. Are you staying?"

Suddenly nervous, I glance once again at his erection and quickly get to my feet, heat coursing through me. "If we're done, I think I'm going to take a break."

He stands with me. "Are you all right?"

I shake my head and turn away. I flee to the house to hide where he can't see how much I want him or how frightened his question makes me.

CHAPTER TWENTY-EIGHT

STRAW, HAY, AND LEAVES

DELILAH

That night, I toss and turn in bed, wondering where Jack is. Does he return to the platform at night? The barn, the stream, the forest?

Is he outside my house? On my deck? Behind my bedroom door? I shift to my side and study the darkness that bleeds into the hallway. There's nothing in sight, but it does little to placate me.

Grumbling, I look at the ceiling, the question of where he sleeps still on my mind.

Reaching across the bed, I wrap my arm around the unused pillow and hug it to my chest. Kicking one leg above my blankets, I listen to the hum of the air unit. My hands clench, unable to shake the pressure of his hand against mine—even through gloves, the tiny contact unlocked something in me.

I still want him.

Closing my eyes with a sigh, my fingers trace over Hollowstalk's necklace strung from my neck.

No. I'm not leaving. Not yet, at least.

And when I do, I won't be returning to San Jose as the same person. Nothing will ever be normal again. Knowing the things I do now, I'll either have to embrace that there's more out there or bury it. Because nobody will ever believe me if I tell them.

I throw off my covers and go to my window. The sky is clear, casting the corn rows in moonlight. As my eyes adjust, a shape appears where Hollowstalk's empty post should be. Not sure what I'm seeing, I squint.

There, rising above the corn *is* Hollowstalk.

Jack.

My heart stutters. All at once, déjà vu strikes.

Curiosity takes hold of me along with something... thrilling. I head downstairs in my nightdress, put on my shoes, and walk outside. I grab the flashlight by the door and scan the sky.

It's clear, the moon bright.

With a final glance at the house to make sure everything is still clear, I point my flashlight forward and step into the first row of stalks, praying I can keep a straight path and reach Hollowstalk.

I just want a glimpse of him. With the flashlight pointed low to the ground, I make the light as small as I can. It darkens, the stalks blocking the moonlight. When the crops give way to the small dirt clearing around the platform, it feels like an eternity has passed. I'm joined only by the chitter of crickets and the flicker of fireflies.

Flicking off my flashlight, I look up at him. Somewhere between Jack and Hollowstalk, his form partially resembles both, neither entirely human nor scarecrow. I climb onto the platform for a closer look.

Eyes glossy and open, they're lifeless, surrounded by Jack's face but with thick stitching trailing the sides of his mouth and up his cheeks. He wears Hollowstalk's old clothes, leaving his muscled chest exposed. Large patches of his skin are segmented by stitching, each formed from a different shade of leather. My fingers twitch at my side.

His dark hair is the same, and so is his height and shape. Crouching to inspect his hands, I'm thankful to find fingers that are human in shape and not a bundle of sticks. His smell is the same—comforting and earthy.

Scanning him over, my eyes are drawn to where his pants hang precariously on his hips. Heavy in shadow yet lightened by moonlight, a bulge grows between his legs.

Heart racing, I look up. Glinting eyes meet mine as Jack unhooks his arms and straightens, towering above me.

"I saw you from my window—"

He cracks his neck and stretches his arms.

My cheeks heat as I turn and climb off the platform. "I just wanted a glimpse."

He steps off with me, managing the distance in a large, balanced step. Even standing on the same level, I still have to crane my neck to see the smirk on his face.

"Why are you smiling now?" I ask, struggling to hold my ground.

"I had a feeling you would come."

My frown deepens as his words sink in, darkness encapsulating his slightly warped features. I glance at his chest, his stitches, his textured skin, and then back to his massive erection. My breathing slows as my nipples peak against the thin cotton of my nightdress.

I take a step back.

He takes a step forward.

I stumble as my back hits the wall of corn.

He slowly leans down. "If you let me kiss you, I will let you leave."

He lifts a hand to pet my hair, brushing the locks that fall over my chest.

"I don't want to leave."

His gaze turns ravenous. And with a flash of teeth, he presses his lips to mine and runs his mouth over me, urging me to kiss him back. Coaxing, urgent, and velvety, his lips cajole me, and I relax into his grip.

Yanked closer, I gasp as he thrusts his tongue between them and takes over my mouth. Pressed hard against his chest, I jump up and straddle his waist when he lifts me. Shifting my hands over his shoulders, they run over the sewn patches of his skin, finding the bumpy texture of his stitching.

He spins me, and my bottom lands on something hard. Perched on the platform's edge, I open my eyes to see Jack stepping away and shrugging off his coat.

My eyes dance over his naked chest as he spreads it out on the platform behind me. Impatient, I grip the tops of his jeans and tug them down. His cock frees with a bounce, jutting hard in front of me.

His hands clench on either side like he has to quell the urge to grab it.

I meet his dark gaze. "Just a kiss," I breathe.

His jaw shifts, and with every limb taut, rubs a section of my hair between his finger and thumb.

I swallow thickly and look down at his swollen cock, hesitating when I recognize the overstuffed middle portion. "Is this..." I break off. No, I don't know why I'm thinking this.

"Is this what?" he rasps, his expression tight.

I cup his member between my hands. "The one you made? Did you sew it onto yourself?"

His head drops back as I stroke him, exploring up and down his softly textured shaft. It's bigger than before, the middle bulkier, but if he did add it to his body, he also could've added length and girth.

Shuddering, he groans. "Yes."

"You sewed it on..." My fingers drift to his base to find the stitches used to attach it.

"Yes."

I pause. "Why?"

"I told you. I wanted to be closer to you."

I should be alarmed at the lengths he is willing to go to for me.

Instead, I want him inside me more than ever.

"You did it... So you could... fuck me?" I ask, shocked.

"Yes," he grits through his teeth, his cock straining in my hands. "If you're afraid I'll do it wrong, *A Cowboy's Seduction* taught me much. I *will* be able to pleasure you."

I want to laugh, but instead, I stare at his overstuffed cock, a cock I've been fantasizing about every night for weeks now. He made it for me...

I need him to know how much I appreciate it.

Licking my lips, I glance up at him. "Did the romance book teach you this?" I whisper, leaning closer to take him into my mouth. All the while, I watch him. He meets my gaze with hunger and fascination as my lips stretch around him, the bulge widening my jaw as I swallow him down.

He moans my name.

Empowered, I pop off and lick along his side, tracing a faint line of stitches there. Slowly, his hands drift to clutch the sides of my head, cupping it. Dropping my eyes, I take him back in my mouth, moving up and down his length.

At the sound of his pleased groan, I slow my rhythm.

"I asked for a kiss?" he asks under his breath. "I should have asked for more."

I smile around him, pull off his length, and give his tip just that.

He shudders again, and for some reason I feel like I've won.

And when I next swallow him down to the sound of his sharp rasp, I know I have.

CHAPTER TWENTY-NINE
A NEW OBSESSION

My jaw strains as Delilah chokes me down.

I never imagined she'd have her lips on my cock or my cock in her mouth.

She holds my gaze as she releases me and softly kisses my cock's tip again. Her tongue travels down and along the stitches on the side. She leans into me and brushes her mouth across the seams around my base, her touch reverent as her dewy tongue dabs my stitch marks.

Bracing and on the verge of snapping, I grip her head as her tongue lavishes. It's too much. Too good. Completely ignorant of my hunger for her, she takes me back inside her throat. Her eyes flick downward, and my fingers tighten on her scalp as the need to thrust increases with every one of her swallows.

When she starts to run her mouth up and down me, I tug her off and lean forward to grab her nape. "Why?" I growl.

Despite needing her answer, I immediately regret pulling her mouth off of my member. Her lips are glistening, stealing my attention. Everything about her is so enticing it hurts. It angers me.

She wipes her hand over her lips. "I wanted more than a kiss."

I stare in stunned silence, as she leans back and wiggles out of her boots, pulling off her short night dress. My necklace hangs loosely from her throat, resting between her small breasts. Lying back onto my coat wearing only her panties, she shifts her butt against the platform's edge. Shifting her thighs apart, she invites me to look.

Her nipples pebble as her chest rises and falls. Unbidden my fingers reach for the last white scrap of fabric hiding her from my view, hesitating only when my finger is clawed around the strap. "I want to see everything."

I pull her panties down.

Straightening, I stare at her.

Wearing nothing except my necklace, I have my queen naked on my platform. With her resting on my coat and among my things, I have never felt so possessive.

Me, a mere scarecrow with a simple purpose, has just been offered his heart's desire.

Quietly watching me, Delilah breathes softly, her naked flesh prickling. I reach down and remove my boots and the pants gathered around them. Stepping up to the platform's edge, I cup her knees and spread them wide, opening her entirely to my view.

Her sex glistens in the moonlight, pretty like flower petals. Gently, I wrap my hands under her butt and move her closer to me, and when my cock bumps against the inside of her thigh, her breath sharpens and she wiggles nearer.

The sweet scent of her arousal floods my nostrils as I rub the tip of my cock between her legs, getting her arousal all over it.

"I like you among my things. I like…" I eye the necklace and nod at it. "That."

She clasps the skull. "Jack…"

I run my tip over her again. "Jack's not here anymore, Delilah."

"Hollowstalk," she says, holding my gaze.

"Good, my queen." Beyond pleased she knows who's about to push inside her. "I need you to know that it's me, Hollowstalk, you're spread for."

"I know who you are," she whispers. "What you are."

Leaning one leg against the platform, I hook her leg upward, spreading her further as I cup her other one with my hand and push it into her chest. "Remind me of what I am."

"A scarecrow."

I take her hand and place it on the fresh stitching on my chest. Gripping her wrist, I slide her palm up my throat and over my cheek where I nuzzle it against the threading at the corner of my mouth. Her expression softens and then heats as I move her hand all over me.

Her touch is bliss, and my body burns with pleasure in the wake of her caress. Shifting her downward, guiding it toward my cock, I rest against her as she cups my rounded shaft with me. Her saliva still coating it, we run her hand along the length of it, leaving me shaking with restraint.

Relaxing her grip, she closes her eyes with a sweet moan as I push forward to slide my tip over her again, testing her entrance, spreading her arousal until we're both wet all over. I pause, admiring how we glisten, how wet she is, and how wet a human can be.

She whimpers and squeezes me, and my head drops in pleasure.

Swallowing thickly, my chin pressed to my chest, I prime my cock against her opening. "I need to feel you around me." I throb for her... *pussy,* a lovely word the cowboy book enlightened me to. To ease my ache, I will push my cock into it—again and again—in every way possible for as long as she accepts it.

"Are you ready?" I reverently touch her opening with my fingers, spreading the new dew gathered there. "Have you prepared?" She's small, and it astonished me at first exploration, causing me to worry if my cock will fit.

She meets my gaze with a slight frown and removes her hand from my cock. Pushing my caressing fingers aside, she swipes her entrance. "We won't know until we try." Her voice is a breathy plea as she dips a finger into herself.

She pulls it out and wipes her slick off on her thigh. Leaning down, I lick it off.

Her legs strain at the touch, my tongue sliding along her skin until I'm between her open legs, tasting her. "Perhaps you should be wetter," I rumble, grazing my teeth along her folds.

She arches her chest, and her hands grab at my head. "Please," she begs.

I grin, my cock stirring to give her what she wants, to know she wants me just as much as I want her. Positioning over her, I guide my tip back to her opening and lean in, resting my hand on the platform as I push into her tightness. Sparks of pleasure burst behind my eyes as her body, at first, accepts me into her.

"My queen." I groan.

She hitches and jerks, gasping as I begin to spear her pussy so slowly it's excruciating. Through winces, whimpers, and moans, I watch her face to know when it's too much.

Little by little, she adjusts, her tense, constricting walls easing as she widens enough to allow me further inside. Dropping my other hand to fist against the platform, I hold back from snapping my hips.

Her little moans and hisses fill my ears as she rocks gently, her heels braced on the edges of the platform. Together, we work me deeper inside her.

I curse myself for making the appendage too large in the middle, wincing with relief and torture as she takes another half-inch.

"You're going to hurt yourself," I grit as the widest part of my girth is clamped at her opening. When I press forward to relieve the pressure, she inhales.

Clenching my jaw, I begin to pull out.

Her grip on me tightens. "No! It's okay."

I stop, my cock immediately wanting to thrust all the way in and end this torment once and for all. One thrust, and it would be done. One thrust, and I'd finally have her.

"Let me try this." She shimmies and rubs her fingers over the nub above where we're joined, running them over it hard. Her eyes hood as she pushes onto me.

I shove her fingers away with a growl. She must need more preparation.

I yank out and drop between her legs and suckle her clit. Her sweet flavor explodes on my tongue, causing my cock to jump. She cries out as I hook her leg over my shoulder and prod her nub. When her hips sail into the air, I force her back to me, impaling her with my tongue.

My tongue works faster. "Say my name," I roar into her. I need to hear it on her lips one more time.

"Hollowstalk, *please!*"

I slip several fingers inside her and stretch them. The moment I do, she freezes.

She's silent as her body constricts, her legs tensing against me. Her sex clamps down as her nails dig into my scalp. Arousal spreads over my hand as some squirts out of her. Lifting my gaze, I find her mouth parted, her eyes squeezed tight.

At the sight of her mindless with pleasure, I reposition between her legs and thrust into her. Her limbs go rigid as her eyes flick open. Her pussy quivers, strangling and accepting me, tearing a pained sound from my throat.

Dropping on top of her, I press my face into her neck and sink deeper until I'm finally seated, her writhing hips urging me on. With her fully stretched around me, I hold prone, taking it all in. Her warmth, the feel of her under me. She's more than I could ever imagine.

She feels like home, far more so than the farm ever has.

Licking her neck, along her throat, and behind her ear, I peer down at her, threading her hair with my fingers.

Her face is both pinched and breathless, her lips parted and wet. "So... full. I've never been so full." She opens her eyes to see me watching her.

I touch her cheek. "I have you. Relax."

She nods, her body easing at its own pace. I wait for her to accept me, soothing her all the while, caressing her cheek and kissing her lips, chin, and along her jaw.

My beautiful queen. I move my hips, pushing deeper and then pulling back. I do it again, watching her face. Her eyes widen as she clutches me, meeting my next shallow thrust with her hips.

I spin us around until she straddles my lap and is impaled upon me.

"Hollow—!"

I meet her mouth with mine, hook my arm around her, and clamp my other hand on her hip, lifting her and tugging her back down. She cries out, and her nails score my chest. Faster, our bodies slam together and tear apart, my cock thrusting as I tug her down and she rears up. Her whimpers become moans and gasps before returning to breathy cries of pleasure. I roll her hips forward and back, feeling her everywhere like I might waste away if I don't.

In the darkness, confined by corn with the night sky above, she takes control with a frenzy, dancing on me. She flings her head back, and I lose my breath at the frantic sight of her riding me with abandon, her long hair bouncing in the moonlight, her teeth biting into her lower lip.

A heavy pounding takes over my senses. She screams out my name so loud anyone could hear, and growling in response, I pull her to me and stuff my tongue in her mouth. Feeling death upon me yet again, I yank her back down as my cock bursts. Her body jerks, expelling a heightened moan of her own. Her sex constricts me deliciously, riding out each shudder with rolling hips. Holding her tight, I flood her with my wetness as she writhes—

She writhes and writhes and, jerking her hips harder, seeks to prolong her pleasure.

I run my hands up and down her back, coaxing her to take what she needs. She can use me as she wants—I will always be ready and willing. There is nothing better in the world than this connection with her.

Breathing hard, Delilah rests her forehead on me. Pleased, I grin as I run my hands over her.

Minutes pass with neither of us moving. On its own accord, my cock hardens and releases inside her again and... when done... It does so again and again, each subsequent climax driving me a little closer to madness. Each time she tenses, straining her pussy around my swollen length.

I want to stuff her with everything I have. I want to fill her with me and only me. I massage her neck and shoulders, her lower back and butt, determined to show her all the ways I want to be close, and I won't have it any other way. She'll be mine for as long as she is here.

Dawn comes far too soon.

The sunlight finds me resting against my pole cradling Delilah, naked and asleep in my arms. Rubbing my hand against my chest, there's a thumping pressure.

I carry her to the house and tuck her into bed.

I look down at her slumbering form, and the pounding in my chest grows. A pounding that wasn't there yesterday. Climbing in with her, I pull her into me.

And wait for her to wake up.

CHAPTER THIRTY

BACK AND FORTH

HOLLOWSTALK

My queen has a wet pussy.

I do everything to keep it that way, preoccupying her in our house until the word satiation means something to me. It's in the romances I read when she sleeps.

Satiation.

If her pussy is wet, it's most likely because she's aroused, and if she is aroused, she lets me inside of her. When I keep her pussy wet, we build intimacy and trust, two things I want more than anything now.

But unlike me, she needs to eat. She needs breaks. And knowing that she is a human and is limited in endurance, I do my best to accommodate her. I feed her fruits and vegetables and have learned to make her coffee, massage her muscles, and make her relaxed. I always give her a chance to rehydrate...

So she can stay wet.

Delilah's moans turn into a whine as she straddles me on a rocking chair, rubbing her brow on my shoulder. My cock tucked inside her, I rock in and out as the chair sways back and forth. In the midday heat, sweat slickens her skin as she grips my shoulders and whimpers, pressing her brow against me.

Keeping our pace slow and steady, I run my hands up and down her spine as her pussy moves over me, tight around my bulge as it slides deeper into her. Fondling her flushed skin, my fingers tangle in her hair. I brace my boots against the deck and spread my thighs wider, opening her up further, coaxing another moan from her throat. Her hold on me tightens as her soles are forced off the ground.

Clutching her hips, I press her down hard the next time the chair tilts upward.

With her naked and shuddering in my lap, I follow each thrust with a long pause. I don't want to take her fast or hard or rough with abandon... Today I want to savor her shudders and gasps.

Sweat beads her brow and glistens across her chest. There, between her peaked breasts, is my crow's skull. My cock jerks, and she releases a quick breath.

Standing while still inside her, I carry her to the den, pull out, and place her over the desk.

She braces her hands, angling herself on the hard surface and spreading her legs. I slide my hands over her back and butt, kneeling behind her. "Good girl."

When I pierce her with my fingers and curl them, she moans, slumping entirely.

I lean in and lick her everywhere my tongue can reach, loving her taste in my mouth. When I pinch her clit with the fingers of my other hand, she seizes, her pussy clamping. Ripping them out, I position over her and push inside.

She quiets as my cock fills her back up. When I'm fully inside, I pinch her clit again.

She rears back, her sheath pulsating. She was closer to her peak than I thought, and holding still, I allow her orgasm to milk me.

Her hips twitch as her release battles with my cock's wide girth. In the struggle, I pin her hips as she writhes, her walls fluttering so hard they're pushing me out.

She looks over her shoulder and glares at me. "Let me move. I need to move."

I scowl but loosen my grip. "Very well."

She faces forward and with a moan, leans back and wiggles her hips, using me to prolong her orgasm. When I try to move, she grumbles, and so I suffer her delicious torture.

When she's done, she lets out an airy laugh and slumps again. "Damn."

Still rigid, I lean over her. "Damn?"

Turning her face to the side, she smiles. "I'm sore."

I lick my lips. "I know."

"Can we take a break now?"

I press into her as I lean down. "I'm not done. But I'll start a bath."

She purses her lips as I release her, pulling out with a frustrated grunt. She slumps further when we come apart. Cupping her sex, I catch a river of my seed as it slips out of her.

"Thank you," she breathes. "That sounds wonderful."

Stepping back, she gingerly lifts and faces me. We look at each other. The only place she's covered is where her long hair falls and where my necklace hangs. Otherwise, we've both been naked since yesterday. Every part of her has been touched by me, some far more than others.

My eyes narrow upon her pinkened breasts, which I have spent ample time pinching because I like it when her nipples are tight. I begin rubbing my cock with my hand.

Her eyes drop, and her lips part. "Still?"

"I can't help it. I need to be inside you." My heart thrums now because of her, and I press my free palm to my beating chest. "I want more."

"Oh. I know." She teases.

Giving my cock a final squeeze, I nod toward the kitchen. "Go grab a drink. I'll be waiting upstairs."

She grumbles again and leaves for the kitchen. Waiting until she's gone, I inhale the scent of our sex, groaning with need.

Cursing when my cock jerks, I almost chase her. Instead, I climb the stairs with speed and prepare the clawfoot tub. By the time Delilah arrives, it's filled with steaming water.

I reach for her hand and drag her into the room. My lips brush her ear as I remove my necklace from around her neck and set it on the counter.

She shivers and takes a slow step into the water. As she lowers, I take her hand, curious why she loves this human ritual of submerging her body.

Settling into the water, she brings her knees to her chest. The water ripples as she closes her eyes with a pleased hum.

I lean against the counter and watch.

"It's strange having you stand over me like that." She sways to the side and faces me. "There's room. Why not join me? You're already naked."

I consider it, my hands twitching to brush her hair off her chest.

"What's wrong?" she asks when I fail to respond.

"My body has never been good with water."

Realization crosses her face. "Do you soak it up?"

"I used to."

"But not anymore?"

"It hasn't been an issue so far—getting my hands in the river or working the sprinklers—but I haven't submerged myself either."

She sits up on her knees and pulls me down to the tub's edge. "Want to test it out?"

Peering down, I stare at the water, reminded of the heaviness it used to curse me with that only the sun could cure.

"You don't have to if you don't want to," she adds. "We can just sit here for a while."

I shake out my hand. "No. I want to." Starting with my fingertips, I sink it into the water, going all the way to my elbow. Warmth closes around me. We wait in silence, and after a moment, I pull my arm out.

"How does it feel?"

"Wet."

She chuckles. "That's it?"

I turn my hand over. "That's it."

I stand and step into the tub, dropping down to sit facing her. Water sloshes over us as she moves onto my lap. My cock settles stiffly between us, the only limb of mine that feels remotely heavy. When her belly brushes my taut patchwork shaft, I lean my back to look at her.

With her long hair wild around her shoulders, and her brown eyes filled with contentment, my chest tightens.

She gives me a sly smile. "I'm going to give you your first bath, Hollowstalk."

I cup her waist with my hands. "Please do."

"Please do... what?" She sits upright.

"Please do, *my queen*," I rasp, suddenly, terribly dehydrated, the insides of my body shriveling. Need hollows out my stomach as I lick my lips.

She laughs some more, pleased by my reaction, and grabs my hands, setting them on the sides of the tub. "It'll be easier if you keep these to yourself."

With gravity, my lips flatten, and I nod, settling back to watch her work.

Twisting away, she grabs a white bottle perched on a raised shelf behind her. With it in hand, she faces me and settles back on my lap and near my cock.

I lick my teeth, making myself ignore the urge to press it against her harder. "I want to be inside you." I shift my legs, enjoying the way her body wiggles and how the water swirls around her.

Unfazed, she squirts the bottle into her hand, readjusting her positioning until she's comfortable. "You have to wait."

I scowl.

Putting the bottle aside, she rubs her hands together creating a frothing lather that she rubs against my chest. Slick with honeysuckle soap, she slides her hands in a circle.

I take in everything she does, aroused beyond measure, charmed by the way she wants to take care of me. This isn't something I'm used to. Nobody has cared for my body outside the barest minimum, enough to keep me whole. The wear and tear I've undergone, the scars of patchwork all over me, is a collection of the care I've received before her. Small wounds fade, but the larger ones will remain with me forever.

Resting my fingers on my newest one, realizing she's been taking care of me from the beginning, my chest constricts.

Delilah's hands pause, and she frowns down at me. "Is it okay?"

"It's fine. I was just thinking how I don't want this one to fade."

"Why not?"

I swipe my finger down the center of her chest and to her navel. "It reminds me of you."

She smiles. "Then I hope it remains too."

She goes back to washing me, and I place my hand back onto the tub's edge. The sensations of hot water and her body straddling mine—her palms running slow movements over worn leather—ease me into a languid state.

Watching her with hooded eyes, I settle into her grooming as the steam rises and her palms explore. They trace my shoulders, arms, and hands. Pausing there, she takes her time, pressing her fingers into me and massaging each joint. I now understand why humans like baths so much.

She shuffles away and has me bend forward and close my eyes. Water is dumped over the back of my head, drenching my hair around my face. When that's over, her fingers thread through my strands as she lathers them.

"You're going to smell so pretty."

"Pretty?"

"Like flowers." She dumps more water onto my head until the bubbles clear away.

"Good. You reminded me of pretty flowers when I saw you in that blue dress."

"You thought I was pretty?"

"You are pretty."

Drifting forward, she straddles my lap again. "I was... kind of hoping you'd notice me and think so."

"Why?"

Delilah breaks her gaze from mine and looks away. "I thought you were attractive. I don't know... I had a crush on you."

"What's a crush?"

"It's the way someone feels when they like someone ro-mantically."

"You mean you fancied me? You were keen on me?"

"*Keen?*" She arches her brow. "Did you learn that from Sylvie's romances?"

I nod.

"Yes then. I *fancied* you."

I consider her. "You wanted to be romantic with me... even then?"

She blushes. "Of course I did. I wanted to go to the festival with you."

"You should have told me."

She meets my gaze. "For the record, I did offer to drive you there. But I suppose you wouldn't have understood flirting. What if I had been more direct, what would you have done?"

"It was at the festival I first considered being your partner. It was then I began to realize why I liked watching you so much. And when that male waved at you..."

She squints. "You saw that?"

"It infuriated me."

My eyes narrow when she bursts with laughter.

"What's so funny?"

"You were jealous!"

I grip her hips and squeeze. "I was jealous. If you were going to have a partner, it was going to be me. There was no way I would accept another's presence being so close to you when it should be me who gets that privilege."

She rests her hands back on my chest. "I was nervous you might have a partner."

"I didn't."

She shifts closer and rises on her knees above my cock. "I know." Reaching between us, she cups my shaft and lowers onto my tip. "No one can do this but me." Seating me inside her, moaning as she stretches to take every inch, I hiss as her pussy squeezes me.

Delilah curls her arms around my neck as her sheath adjusts to accept me. When she begins to quiver against me, I pull her to my chest and hold her.

Her hips slowly circle.

She moans against my ear.

She speeds up.

Her nails dig into my shoulders.

I groan, maddened with lust as she dances with my cock.

With steam and heat enveloping us, she dances and dances and dances, crumbling my mind and working my body into a taut fervor.

I clutch her waist, unable to hold back any longer, and cut through her tempo with a firm thrust. Water spills from the tub, and she gasps, straightening up on me just in time for the next thrust.

Water splashes around her as she cries out.

"No one can do this but me," I repeat her words back to her, thrusting harder while clutching her waist. Knowing what I know now, I'd run my scythe through anyone who tried to take my place.

I need her to feel that it's me inside her and nobody else. I snap my hips as my thrusting roughens, forcing her to jerk upward as I ride up into her.

She winces, parting her mouth.

"I would have you like this... like this in a blue dress," I growl.

A gaspy, breathless moan leaves her, and encouraged, I impale her faster until her abrupt climax traps my member. In a frenzy to join her, I bury myself, fighting her now constricting, strangulating walls.

When she cries out my name again, her mouth against my ear, I come undone. Going rigid on my next thrust, I trap her in my trembling limbs and back down into the tub where I keep her exactly where I want her as I flood her with seed.

I pet her as we relax, my body emptying into her. Her breathy moans fill my ears as what water remains settles around us.

"See, water isn't so bad after all," she whispers.

"It's much better."

Delilah gingerly sits up. Her long, wet hair is tangled around her shoulders, the moist strands curling on her skin. She runs her fingers along my stitches, and as she studies them, she yawns.

Pulling her back against me, I hold her until her breathing lengthens.

And as the water slowly grows cold, I pray this moment never ends.

CHAPTER THIRTY-ONE
THE VISITOR

DELILAH

It's August.

When did it become August?

Time is slipping away, and as dawn's first light seeps through the curtains, I drift back to sleep before I remember this is temporary.

When I next stir, it's to the warmth of Hollowstalk's body beneath my cheek. I shift my ear over his chest and listen to his heartbeat, still bewildered that it's there. He's changed since I sewed him closed. I skim my fingers over the stitches on his chest.

While I'm doing that, he's caressing my nipple, running lazy circles with his thumb. "Morning," he hums as he lifts his eyes to mine.

"Morning..." I inch my hand down his stomach, along his hip bone, finding his cock. Primed and hard, precum drips from the tip. I squeeze and tug at him.

He groans, and before I can slide my hand over him, he turns me over and settles me on the pillow. With my butt suddenly raised his tongue presses between my legs, tracing my inner lips until he stops... *there.*

Like an artisan, he teases the orgasm from my body.

Over the days, I have gone from sore to healed and sore again as I take him, *all of him*, time and time again.

I'm dreamy and delirious as he positions his cock between my butt cheeks, squeezing them together as he thrusts over and between them. I'm too sore to take him again and if it didn't feel so good, I would have asked him for a break sooner.

He rasps my name and straddles me, his thrusting turning frantic. The bed rattles as his hands come down on either side of me and he jerks forward at his next thrust. His restraint snaps, and he releases it all over my back.

His thrusting ceases with his climax, and I shift onto my back, smearing his cum on the sheets to look up at him.

His patchwork skin is on display. The stitching on his face is easy to see.

He grins down at me.

"I should probably wash the sheets."

"But then they'll smell like soap."

"And what should they smell like?"

"Us."

Shaking my head, laughing, I sit up higher, only then realizing he's still staring at his cum spread across the bedding. "What is it?"

"I'm still curious what this is—" he runs a finger along it "—and why I'm making it."

Swallowing, I try to forget I'm having frequent and unprotected sex. I've always wanted children, but his seed is nothing like human semen, right? It's slicker, I think, and it tastes rich, like caramel. "And I wonder why you now have a heartbeat."

"You know it has to do with you."

I'm afraid of that.

We shower, dress, strip the bed, and I find he's right—it's a little sad. The sheets might be a rumpled mess, but it's a mess that we've made.

Bundling them up, I head downstairs and pause in the kitchen to make coffee while I start the washer. Afterward, I find Hollowstalk inspecting the fields from the front porch, and I join him with a steaming mug cupped in my hands. In the cool morning air, I hug my coffee close.

He busted out the radio and set it to the public station's morning jazz. The songs are old, and I don't know most of them, but he loves them. Whenever jazz plays, he tracks every note, his expression one of stern concentration as he listens carefully.

With a twinkle in his eyes, he notices me. Heading my way, he takes my coffee and sets it aside. He pulls me into his arms and spins me to the music.

Laughing, we dance.

The sunlight underlines his warm skin and gives his dark brown hair a golden sheen.

I'm still amazed by the wonder that he is. Crow's Rest's creepy scarecrow is nothing like I first thought.

I like him.

A lot.

A lot more than I should like someone who can fade away.

I pull from his arms. "Thank you for the dance."

He tips his head, eyeing me curiously.

"How's the corn?" I peer around him and across the field.

"The corn is fine. Come, I'll show you."

He helps me stand and together we head to the nearest stalks. Grabbing a cob, he rips it off and faces me. Pulling back the husk and silks, Hollowstalk breaks the corn in two, handing me a piece.

The kernels are fully formed, though small and the palest of yellows. They're firm and underripe.

"They'll be ready to harvest in about a month."

My brain stutters as I frown up at him. "Really? That soon?"

"Yes." His curious expression returns. "Is there something wrong with that?"

"I... don't know." Fiddling with the crow skull hanging from my neck, I look back at the house and tally what's left to be done. "As long as everything is in order... It's nothing."

"If you say so." He arches a brow. "I'm going to check the crops today, clearing them of pests. It may take me much of the day. Unless you would like me to stay?"

"Painting the shed should be easy." I smile up at him. "I've got it."

"Shout if you need me." He studies me for a moment, and I pretend not to notice. When he saunters away, my throat grows tight, and I look back down at the broken cob.

A month. That's not very long.

I've been skirting around having *the* conversation with him.

I'm not staying forever. This is temporary. I have a job back home, and I want to return to it. I can't run a farm for the rest of my life, the isolation will kill me. But I'm also too afraid to bring it up, scared that I might ruin something wonderful.

By noon, I'm frazzled and covered in sweat and specks of red paint. Thankfully, the shed is finally done and stands out amongst the garden, bringing out the colors of the flowers. I'm searching for any spots that may need another coat when I hear the rumble of a car rolling down the road. I squint to see who it is as they turn into the driveway.

Miranda?

I wave as she parks and steps out of her car. Opening the back, she pulls out several mason jars.

Her expression turns doubtful as I approach her. "I hope I'm not intruding. I was dropping these off at a friend's down the road, and since I had extras, I thought I would offer them to you. Homemade salsa, and one of my best recipes," she adds with a twinkle in her eye.

"You're fine. I'm just finishing up a project." My shoulders relax. "And, yes, please, salsa sounds great! I'm about to have lunch. Would you care to join me?"

I want to stay on her good side and learn if I can trust her.

I can't just sell the farm to anyone, not anymore.

"I'd love to." She hands me the jars. "I have some chips too, if you're interested in cracking one of these open."

"You're amazing. Thank you."

She returns to the car, and I plaster a smile on my face, almost wishing Miranda weren't so nice. *Almost.* It's sweet, knowing she's looking out for me. Even if it is just chips and salsa. It's these little bits of human connection that keep me grounded. Out here there haven't been many, and I've come to cherish the little things.

I don't want to hurt her.

"I'll be right back." I duck inside, drop off the extra jars, wash my hands, and grab two bowls from the cupboard.

By the time I'm back and setting everything on the outdoor table, Miranda is at the edge of the cornfield, looking at the stalks. She eyes the house and joins me on the deck. "You've done a great job. It's beautiful here."

She opens a bag of tortilla chips as I pour the salsa into the bowls. Eagerly, I take my first bite, finding the salsa sweet and spicy and absolutely delicious.

Miranda picks up a chip and scoops up her salsa, giving me an expectant smile.

My shoulders tighten. While she's friendly, I'm pretty sure this is a business call. "We can schedule a date to talk specifics." The words burn my throat.

"That sounds great. I can see you're almost done."

This is great news. It should be. I have a buyer. Miranda's the type of person who just might hear me out and even *want* the blessing of a... crow god.

"How are you holding up?" she asks, breaking me from my thoughts.

"Sorry. I'm okay. Your salsa is so good that I got distracted." It's not a lie. "You told me once my aunt sold you corn each fall?"

She shifts in her seat. "Every fall for the past twenty-two years. I'm going to miss her."

"Can I ask what you knew about my aunt? I'm learning she was... that maybe..."

"She was a witch?"

"You... know?"

"Sweetheart, everyone knew." Miranda laughs and settles deeper in her chair, a crease forming on her brow as she eyes my necklace. "I was in the same book club as Sylvie, and she would always bring something from her gardens, claiming everything she grew was blessed." Miranda shrugs. "Everything she grew always turned out good, so maybe it was."

I smile. "Yeah, I've learned some of that from Jack."

"Jack?"

"My field hand. He's the guy helping me."

"Oh, right! Jack. He's an interesting fellow, that one."

"You know Jack?"

"We spoke at the midsummer festival about the property being up for sale. I'm sorry if I forgot to mention it. I haven't thought about it since then."

"He mentioned the farm was going up for sale?" I ask, even more confused. We both talked to Miranda at the festival? He never mentioned he did more than follow me.

She laughs. "He said he wanted me to buy it."

My heart drops.

"Anyway—" Miranda waves "—your aunt never said much, especially after Ivar died, but when she did speak, she told the best stories."

"I wish I knew her."

And I wish I knew why Hollowstalk wants you to have the farm.

Because I can't help thinking our reasons aren't the same.

CHAPTER THIRTY-TWO
FRAYED EMOTIONS

DELILAH

After she's gone, I wring my hands, pacing the deck.

How does she know his name? He told me not to worry if the pact was broken, that he would be fine, but the more I think about it, the more I'm concerned. I know he can't take direct ownership—he was made to aid the land, not own it—so why would he approach someone like Miranda on his own accord?

The thought turns my stomach to acid.

The sky is darkening and the fireflies start to appear by the time I spot Hollowstalk emerging from the cornstalks.

When he walks onto the porch and leans his scythe on the banister, I can't keep it in any longer. "She knew you."

He hesitates. "Who?"

"Miranda."

His face goes blank. "I met her at the festival."

"When you went looking for me?"

"I was also looking for someone to take over..." he trails off.

"A new queen?" I whisper.

His face hardens, and he reaches for my wrist. "Things are different now."

I pull away before I show him how wrapped up in him I've become. "It's all right. She would care for Crow's Rest and... I have to go back home."

He scowls. "No. You don't. You don't have to go anywhere."

"You've had many queens. What's one more?"

Cupping my cheeks, he forces me to look up at him. "I have had many queens and none of them, not even Winifred, gave me a heart. As long as I fulfilled my purpose, I was ignored. None of them were you. None of them could ever be you. *You* sparked my interest. You've sparked everything."

I want it to be true, to be as good as he thinks I am.

And I think the doubt shows on my face, the glimmer of moisture in my eyes.

He kisses me gently, his soft lips moving over me. I don't respond, unable to think. I'm too afraid to kiss him back.

But he doesn't allow me to remain frozen for long, trapping me against the front door and pressing his cock against me.

Only one month until harvest.

Gasping, I tug off his shirt, running my hands up his chest. My palms slide, bumbling against his taut threads. Leather, skin, and burlap, the texturing of his flesh wavers under my touch.

"You're my queen," he groans against the side of my lips.

Attacking him with a nip and sighing in his arms, I come undone.

I unbutton my jeans, and he wrenches them past my hips, taking my underwear and shoes too. I grip his pants and do the same, tugging them down his thighs. His member springs forth, thicker in the middle than I've ever seen before, causing my mouth to water and my breath to halt.

Soreness be damned. I still want him.

He slides his fingers between my legs, and they come away wet and slick. Capturing my gaze, he licks them and swipes them once more between my legs, making my hips jerk. "You're perfect." He licks his fingers again, and when he presses them to my pussy once more, he doesn't swipe like before—he pushes them into me.

He curls them inward, and I whimper.

"This—" he leans into me, his tall frame blocking everything else out "—is why you should stay."

My lips part.

Pulling his fingers out, he presses my back against the door, lifting me at the same time. Pinning me at an angle, he impales me on his cock. I cry out and grip him, clenching wildly around his added girth. Without any of his languid foreplay, he thrusts upward, pushing me up the door and stuffing me, as if I could possibly take more of him.

I bury my face into his neck as he comes, squeezing me in his near-strangling embrace. Holding me upon him, he backbends at a sharp angle and watches his cock twitch, stretching me a little more with each pulse.

"Hollowstalk," I breathe, on the edge of my own release, awed by his weird angle, one that would be impossible for a human. His gaze flicks to mine, and straightening, he pulls out, letting his cum spill down my legs and onto the welcome mat.

Gasping, I don't get a moment to breathe before he picks me up and lowers me onto the porch.

Spreading my thighs as wide as he can, he spears me with three quick thrusts. It's all I need to unravel with a scream. With his hands on either side of my head, he holds prone above me, watching me with such intensity that I close my eyes to focus on riding each powerful wave. My legs clamp around his hips, trapping him there as the pulsing continues, desperate for it to never end.

A short time later, we lie on the deck, resting under the porch light and listening to the crickets. I snuggle in the crook of his arm as his fingers play with my hair.

Touching my lips with my finger, I think they're bruised.

I don't mean to think about my day or the strange conversation with Miranda...

His petting hesitates. "What is it?"

"Nothing."

"Really?"

I name the nearest, closest topic. "I was thinking about Miranda's salsa."

"Miranda." He rises onto his elbows, his eyes narrowed on me. "You're considering selling her the farm, aren't you?"

He glares at me like I've done something wrong—like I don't have a choice in the matter. My spine straightens as I sit taller, searching around for my clothes. "She knew Sylvie was a witch, and I don't think anything about this place will surprise her."

His jaw tightens.

I continue, "You picked her yourself... And I'll make your employment part of the contract."

He stares at me in bewildered silence.

I search for something, anything better to say, but nothing comes to mind. My tongue feels too thick for my mouth. How do I tell Hollowstalk, a scarecrow, someone who has never left the property that this isn't fair? None of it's fair.

When I don't continue, he stands and searches for his clothes too. "I told you," he snaps. "You don't need to worry about me."

"I always planned on selling." I turn on him. "You knew that."

He throws his arm out toward the fields. "Look around you. What are you searching for that isn't already here? You have food, shelter, privacy, protection—"

"I…" I catch my breath, swallow, and try not to drown.

He takes a step toward me. "—you have me!"

I move away, unable to meet his eyes. "I don't know what I'll do."

He searches my face, and whatever he sees there makes him shake his head. "That makes two of us."

My brow furrows as he turns away and walks off the porch.

"Hollowstalk…" I wish there were a way to make him understand, to say this isn't easy for me. That if I commit to this place and something happens to him…

I clench my fists and stop myself from chasing him.

And with his name hanging in the air, he strides into the darkness, vanishing within the field's shrouded depths.

CHAPTER THIRTY-THREE

REDEYES

DELILAH

He's gone the rest of the day. And the next, only appearing long enough to fuss with equipment, barely acknowledging me when I try to make conversation.

I'm starting to grow annoyed.

What does he expect me to do? *Stay?* How could a relationship between us last?

He's not even human.

He can't come with me when I leave.

Looking around the dining room, I take in all the updates. There's not much left to do.

What had once seemed like an impossible task is now almost complete. Everything I've set out to accomplish this summer is nearly done. I've tended to my aunt's history, rebuilt her house, and now... I'm bored.

Reaching up, I play with the crow's skull dangling around my neck. I'd expected to be excited when I got to this point, not suffering dread.

It's eerily quiet, and it's almost a relief when the next sip of my coffee is interrupted by several caws outside the front window.

Ignoring it, I turn the page in my book, but the crow cries out again.

And again.

Sighing, I shuffle in my seat to see what's happening outside the window. Redeyes stares back at me from where he's perched on the railing.

He caws louder.

Curious, I stand and open the window. He hops along the deck rail and away from me. "Hi," I say. He cocks his head and calls out again.

Right then, Hollowstalk appears from the side of the house. Wearing his hat and coat and carrying his scythe, he looks like he walked straight out of a horror story. It's not often he's in full scarecrow attire.

He spares a glance for me and, upon seeing the bird, hesitates. Redeyes takes off and flies away.

"That was strange," I watch the crow vanish into the forest.

"He's not dangerous, not anymore," he says.

For a moment, our eyes connect, and while I'm not sure who looks away first, I hope it's not me. I want him to say more.

Anything.

He turns and walks away. Fidgeting with the sill, I close the window.

The next morning, Redeyes is back, and it all happens again. He caws, gets my attention, and leaves. When he calls out for the third morning in a row, I research how to befriend crows and go into town to buy a bag of mixed nuts. The next morning I pour them into a bowl, set the bowl on the deck's edge, and back away.

He hops onto the porch and prods the treats with his beak.

"They're nuts," I explain. "The internet said you'd like them. They're probably not as good as *blessed corn*," I give him air quotes, "but it shouldn't be bad either. I never meant to worry you. I didn't know about the pact, and my aunt didn't warn me." I know he can't understand me, but I pretend he gets the gist. "The corn will be ready soon. I hope it's tasty."

He blinks and turns back to the dish, finally snacking on my offering. He cleans the bowl and flies away.

The next morning, it happens again. The third time, I hover a little closer.

He's not so intimidating after all.

This time when he finishes the nuts, he doesn't fly off. He ponders me instead.

Finally.

"Hi," I breathe. "I'm Delilah."

He gives a low caw.

"Is it okay that I've been calling you Redeyes?" I ask.

He caws.

"I'll take that as a yes."

He chatters, giving the bowl a final, thorough inspection before flying off.

I may have made a new friend.

More days pass, and with each one, he appears. It's a small victory, but I cling to it because, in every other regard, I'm increasingly agitated.

Not sure what else to do, I turn my attention to weeding the garden. One by one, I tug them out, shaking off the dirt from their roots and adding them to my growing pile of waste.

A caw sounds, and I look up to see Redeyes perched on the shed. It's the first time he's sought out my attention when it isn't morning.

I stand and take a small, hesitant step toward him. When he doesn't move, I take another. Step by step, I approach him. Once I'm within arm's length, he lifts his head and shakes out his wings.

"May I pet you?"

He caws and shimmies.

Reaching out slowly, I gently run my hand down his back. "You're very soft."

At the sound of footsteps, Redeyes flies to the shed. Hollowstalk appears, once again holding his scythe.

"You shouldn't be making a pet out of the Crow King's emissary," he scolds

"I've just been giving him snacks. What's the harm in that? And for the record, he came to me."

Hollowstalk glares at the bird.

Redeyes chitters like an embarrassed child and flies off.

Brushing off the dirt, I stand up. "You scared him away."

"That's my *job*." He closes the span between us, crowding over me, coming the closest we've been in weeks. "Why do you bother befriending a bird when you intend to leave?"

Confused, my mouth opens and closes. "I..."

His yellow eyes are punishing, sharp enough to penetrate my soul. "I?" he prompts.

I shake my head, and to my disappointment, he walks away.

CHAPTER THIRTY-FOUR

RETURN TO THE WINDMILL

HOLLOWSTALK

I glare as the emissary follows Delilah around the farm. Unless he's bored or hungry, he rarely leaves her side. I clench my hands and head back to the windmill despite every thread in my body wanting to drive the crow away.

My teeth grit.

She doesn't realize how great my need for her is.

Running my hands along the smooth wood, I check the board one more time for roughness. This will not work if it causes any discomfort. For the past several days I have hidden away in the old windmill, cleaning it, repairing it, and crafting a new pole from the excess wood of one of Delilah's projects.

It looks like mine, only smaller and newer, with a flush middle for her back to rest against. The corn-stalk ties are fresh and braided, hanging from the side arms. Taking them in my hands, I test their strength once more.

Delilah keeps trying to talk to me.

I've tried to stay away—not anymore.

It's been weeks since I last entered her, and my patience has worn thin. Nothing in the anatomy book told me this would happen. What was meant as a physical partnership has morphed into something bigger. Something that maddens me at the thought of her departure. The mere thought of it seizes my throat. And no matter how many times I close my eyes and shake my head, trying to shake *her* out, it doesn't work.

I thought if I distanced myself, the idea of her leaving would be easier to accept, but after weeks of trying, I still couldn't get her out of my head.

Finally, I saw the issue. I want a lot more than *talk* from her. In romance books, love is what the characters seek from one another, what they win by the end of each story. I'm not sure why I didn't realize it sooner, the books have been there all along, telling me exactly what is happening.

Double checking that the pole is secured against the wall, I straighten the rug beneath it. When I'm done, I peel off my leather gloves and toss them aside.

Everything's ready.

I leave the windmill behind and approach the house. The emissary watches me from his newly found perch on the deck's roof.

"Leave us," I growl.

He caws and flies off.

When he's gone, I pause and listen at the front door, hearing a faint noise within. The handle gives way, the door swinging inward slowly. Keeping my steps quiet, I find Delilah in the kitchen folding towels from a laundry basket, the radio playing music beside her. Her back is to me as she stacks the towels on the counter.

Wearing a loose T-shirt and shorts, her legs are bare to her upper thighs. Her wild brown hair is tied high on her head, its ends drifting over her shoulders. Her clothes hide as much as they reveal. My cock throbs harder, my finger twitching to reach up her shirt.

She still doesn't notice me as she partially turns in my direction and neatly places the towels in the cabinet by the sink.

I clear my throat. "I need you to look at something."

She startles and pivots to face me, placing her hand on her chest. Her cheeks redden, and her brow furrows as her eyes run over me. She takes a breath. "You scared me."

"It's in my nature."

We stare at each other, her expression shifting between curiosity, worry, and hesitancy.

"What is it?" she asks when I don't offer more.

I head back outside. "Follow me." I don't have to look over my shoulder to know she's there.

"Where are we going?"

"The windmill."

"Is it the stairs again?"

"No."

She doesn't say anything more as we make our way toward the windmill's open doors, and I'm glad. I don't want to lie to her.

Stepping inside the old structure, I turn and face her as she walks in after me. Her gaze flicks around the large space, landing back on me before she notices the pole. Once it captures her attention, she stares at it.

The late afternoon light haloes behind her, making the contour of her form glow with gold. The bright light bleeds into her tied-up hair, and my gaze hungrily traces the column of her neck and down where the light allows me to see her body through her shirt.

"You are so beautiful," I groan, unable to hold the words in.

She looks at me and crosses her arms over her stomach. A rosy color spreads across her cheeks that makes me hungry for the taste of strawberries. "I don't understand what's happening between us."

I bow my head. "I'm going to tell you the truth. I want you to love me."

Her gaze shifts over my face. I let my human features fade away until my face is nothing more than cloth and thread, barely recognizable as a man's. Cracking my neck, everything tightens, and I straighten just as quickly.

She's quiet while I reveal my true nature to her again.

"Will you consider it?" I ask.

"I... I have considered it. Do you—" She licks her lips. "Can you feel love?" she whispers.

"I believe I can." I reach out and brush back her hair, and when she doesn't flinch, I close the rest of the distance between us. "I believe I do," I lower my voice and take her wrist, bringing it to my lips and kissing it. "I tried to stay away, tried to make this feeling disappear, for your sake and mine. It didn't work." I cup her chin and lift it. "I don't want to talk to you, and I don't want to listen. I already know what you're going to say and how I will respond. It took time, but now I know nothing is going to change with distance. Not for me at least."

"What are you saying?"

"I'm selfish." I brush my lips over hers. "I've made you some-thing." I step aside.

She looks past me and at the pole. "A scarecrow's pole?"

"Your pole. I've been in your world all this time. I thought I would show you mine."

"How?" There's a soft tremble in her voice.

I take her wrist and lead her to my creation, pressing against one of the arms. "I'm going to bind you."

After a moment's hesitation, she nods and allows me to continue, watching me as I take her arm, her heart racing hard enough for me to hear.

I try to be gentle as I tie it to the post.

In silence, I bind her other wrist. With her hands slightly above her head and to her sides, she looks at each of them. As I had hoped, it's a good height for her—elbows bent and arms slack, she stands tall with the center beam in position to help support her weight.

Her body will be easy to maneuver up and down at will...

Her flesh turns crimson as I decide what to do next, suddenly overwhelmed by choices.

Kneeling, I remove each of her shoes, setting her bare feet against the soft rug.

I memorize every detail.

"What are you doing now?" she breathes, thrill—or perhaps fear—edging her voice.

Even frightened, she allows me liberties.

I run the back of my fingers over her cheek, soothing her as her response arouses me. "What I've wanted to do these past weeks." Placing my hand on her shoulder, I press her back. She gasps and remains rigid. Her hooded gaze searches mine, her feet shifting closer together. I return to petting her. "You'll always have power over me, that will never change."

She swallows and nods, urging me to continue.

"But here—" I reach up and grab her bound wrist, squeezing it, clamping my other hand around the back of her neck to tug my necklace against her throat. "I have all the power. Do you understand what I'm doing now?"

Her lips part. "Yes." Her fingers curl inward.

"Good, my queen." I smile.

Resting back against the pole, she finally relaxes. "I missed you."

I shrug off my coat. "I missed you too."

Letting it drop to the ground, I tug off my boots and unbutton my pants. My cock springs free, so overstuffed the discomfort has been relentless. She doesn't know I've nearly ripped my cock off, trying fruitlessly to ease the ache.

Her eyes glaze over, locked on my appendage. I press against her and lick her throat, earning a moan. Biting her ear, I grind into her stomach.

She shifts her legs apart. "You don't need to wait."

I grab her hand and form it into a fist, knocking her knuckles against the wood behind her. "Do that if you need me to stop."

"Okay." She writhes. "But I can't do that if you don't start."

"Show me. Knock on the wood so I know you can."

"Fine." She does as I say. "There. I'll do that if I need you to stop—"

I stuff my fingers in her mouth, and she gapes with surprise. Sliding them all over her tongue and getting them wet, I return her gaze.

She bites down, and I tug my fingers free with an unamused grunt. Grabbing her shorts, I rip them off and push my hand into her underwear to probe her opening.

I shove my fingers inside of her. Her hips wiggle with each thrust as I shove them in and out.

When she's drenched, I grab her legs and hook them over my shoulders. She slides up the pole as I clutch her thighs and hold her weight. Running the blunt side of my tongue along her thigh, some of my threads snap, breaking as my stomach hollows out with hunger.

True burning hunger. The kind only strawberries and pussy can sate.

Shoving her panties aside, I position between her legs and sink my tongue inside her.

She arches her hips. "Oh, god."

But I'm the one in control. Not some god.

Looking up at her, I scowl, refusing to give her more. She thrashes harder, her way of begging.

I pull my tongue out. "Shh," I say, my gaze slipping between her legs. "You don't get to decide anymore."

She grows quiet, and I half-expect her to knock against the pole and force me to stop... but she doesn't. "Okay," she accepts, still giving me a pleading look.

Baring my teeth and giving in, I rip her panties away and lap everywhere, licking until she's back to writhing on my face mindlessly.

"Love me, Delilah." I press my mouth against her sweet opening. "Love me, and I will give you everything. Everything I can give."

Her arms strain at her sides. "*Hollowstalk!*"

Sliding her down, I unhook her legs from my shoulders and help her stand. I seize her shirt, splitting it down the middle and tossing the remnants aside. I step back and sigh, greedily taking in her naked and bound form. Wearing only my necklace, my queen is sublime on her pole.

"Hollowstalk."

This time, she groans my name with frustration.

I set my foot between hers, forcing her legs further apart and then grab her waist, lifting her so she stands on her toes. "Lean back," I instruct.

The angled pole performs as designed, giving me extra leverage, and I rub the tip of my cock between her legs. She's gasping for breath as I nudge her opening wide, spreading her wetness over me. "Love me," I growl.

I push inside.

She buckles as I sink in, forcing her to take my girth and my length. But she cushions me so tight, I'm nearly pushed out. Groaning, drifting my eyes closed, I tremble, digging my fingers into her flesh as I keep my cock planted. "It's been too long," I rasp.

She moans in agreement, her face flinching as her pussy accommodates me.

My gaze meets hers when she opens her eyes. We stare at each other, our ragged breaths matching.

She leans closer, and her tongue skates over my lower lip.

I cup her throat and shove my mouth to hers, filling her in my two favorite ways, nudging my hips upward. She breaks the kiss and drops her head back. When I straighten and jerk my hips again, her next gasp is louder still. She cries out in pleasure again.

My restraint shatters, and I lean back and thrust. And thrust. *And thrust.*

The pole wobbles as I explode.

I take her on a pole like the one I've been trapped on for nearly two hundred years. I grip her as she slides up and down with each one of my measured thrusts. Pressing my face into her neck, my movements sharpen feeling the edge near. Her quiet gasping fills my ears with the sound of creaking wood.

She's no longer begging for more when I slow down, and I grin, knowing she's finally submitted. She's going to let me play. She's giving me power over her, and unless she protests, I'll be the one to decide how this ends.

So, I make love to my queen for hours, enjoying every single moment.

The day darkens to twilight as I lazily pump in and out of her. I bend my body at an inhuman angle so I can lick her nipples, liking how her tight peaks feel against my tongue. Later, I kneel before her, and lap her pussy until she drips and her nub is swollen.

I try to break her with intimacy, I try to burrow so deep inside her that I'll never come out again.

We've been at this for so long, her wetness slicks the pole. She can barely stand, and her muscles quiver under my circling palms.

Clutching her to me, I thrust once more.

"Hollowstalk," she moans my name, her face flushed, her body glistening with sweat and her hair plastered to her skin. "I need…"

I arch my brow. "You need?"

She licks her lips. "Water."

Releasing her gently to lie against the pole, she shudders and relaxes against it to peer at me through her lashes.

She breathes.

I wait for her to say more, to beg.

She doesn't.

Smiling, I head into the house and fill several bottles. When I return, I hold them to her mouth until she takes what she needs, watching me all the while.

I push back between her legs as she drinks, as her throat bobs and water escapes to trickle down her chin. Lodging my cock back inside her, her walls constrict around me with each subsequent swallow.

I groan and clutch at her hair with my free hand. "Do you understand now what it's like?"

I lower the bottle.

"Yes," she gasps, breathless. "I do."

Reaching up, I untie her wrists. She slips off the pole and into my arms, and I hold her against my chest. The crows watch us as I carry her outside and into the yard. In the first shimmer of moonlight, I lie her out on the grass.

She moans and stretches as I kneel over her. Behind me, the shadow of the Crow King rises over us.

Entering her once more, I finally allow myself to empty inside her, and when I'm depleted of everything I have, I run my lips all over her naked body and kiss every inch of her flesh, while I soothe her aches with my hands. When she's lulled close to sleep, I spread her legs once more and, dabbing my tongue, coax out one final, gentle orgasm from her. She quivers and watches me with hooded eyes until they drift closed and she falls asleep.

I pull Delilah against me as I lie back on the grass.

"She is good to you," I hear the Crow King say from somewhere off in the darkness.

"She is," I agree.

Agitated by his invasive presence, I stand and gather Delilah in my arms. I carry her away from his shadow and into the house where she can no longer be seen.

CHAPTER THIRTY-FIVE
A NEW THREAT

DELILAH

I stare at the pole. *My pole.*

He made it just for me. The morning rays strike the room, casting the space in a different light than the afternoon before. A warmer mood that eases any doubt I had about my decision to let him tie me up yesterday. He had power over me, and I succumbed to it. *He makes me feel safe.*

I've largely ignored the windmill since my incident with the stairs, but Hollowstalk has brought new life to a space that was dark and drafty. Old rugs cover the floor, and the stairs have been replaced. There's a panel with paint on the wall, and another with a wall hanging. They're all things I thought I threw out, things that he must have saved.

I swallow, returning my attention to the pole, the focal point of the room.

Walking forward, I pick up the strap and rub its smooth surface between my fingers. I roll my wrist, flexing my hand, feeling it out. My skin isn't raw. My shoulders are tight, but it's not unreasonable, considering...

He wants me to understand him. He wants me to know what it's like to have the world happen to me, being subjected to the whims of others.

He wants me to love him...

I hear his footsteps approach me from behind and turn around to find Hollowstalk crowding the doorway. Upon seeing me, he closes the distance between us.

"Still sore?" He presses at the knot in my shoulder.

"Yeah, a little," I say. "Us humans aren't built like scarecrows, I suppose."

He presses the knot harder. "Does it hurt you, when I do that?"

"It's uncomfortable but working on it now will help me recover."

"And that's your job, isn't it, helping people with their bodies?"

"Yeah."

"And you want to return to this work? More than you want to stay with me"

"I like helping my patients. But it's mostly about being social."

He switches to my other shoulder. "There aren't many people on a farm."

"No. And it's a career I've chosen for myself. My mom always told me kinesiology was unladylike, but I was determined and won a scholarship of my own." I face him. "How are the fields?"

"The corn is ready to be harvested. I'll start Friday."

I frown. "That's only a couple of days away. That's earlier than I expected."

He nods, his expression giving nothing away. "The weather has been good."

Shifting on my feet before I panic, I look around. "What happens on harvest day? Do I need to prepare?"

"Are you interested in participating?"

"I might be." I can't help being curious.

For a moment he goes silent, considering it. "I had planned to do it all… But there isn't much to it. First, we call on the emissary and tell him it's time. He will then go tell his flock. The next morning, they will swarm the fields and take their share."

"That's it?"

"That's it. Each of the previous pactholders have ritualized it in their own way. Your aunt would cook an elaborate meal."

I frown. "Guess I thought there would be more spectacle to it."

His expression turns wistful. "There was a celebration the first year. I was newly made…" he trails off like he's lost in the memory.

"Tell me about it."

"It was a festive night. I know that now. But at the time all I could do was watch from the sidelines, curious but unable to partake. I've since wondered how it would be to truly celebrate."

"We'll have a party on Friday then. I promise." Even to me, it sounds like a farewell party, and my words hang between us. "What was Winifred like? From reading her journal, I'm not sure if I respect or fear her."

"Like most of the women who became queens of Crow's Rest, Winifred was a woman of her own mind, frightfully determined and circumspect of those who might drive her to ruin. She created me so I might guard her work, ensuring that her labor came to fruition. But I was only that to her, a doll bewitched to her bidding, another of the many enchantments she weaved during her life." Thoughtful, he looks at his hand, fist clenching and relaxing. "For all her ambition, I don't know what she would think if she saw me now."

I lift a hand to his chin, turning his face to mine. "For what it's worth, I think you're magnificent."

He smiles, then frowns, and I understand his unspoken plea—if he is so wonderful, why is it so difficult for me to stay?

Pulling his arm over my shoulder, I lean into him, pressing my ear to his chest so I might listen to the thump of his heart. No matter what happens between us, I want him to keep it beating.

Even if I can't stay, I need to know he'll be okay.

Later that day, I try to keep my focus on the road ahead.

My fingers tap on the steering wheel as I turn onto the highway that leads into town. Forest and farmland pass me by, snagging my gaze with their changing colors. The wind picks up, violently rustling their branches, already forcing leaves to fall.

When another gust shoves my truck to the side of the lane, my grip on the wheel tightens.

Friday.

There isn't much time left, and I need to tell Miranda everything.

Raindrops splatter on my windshield, and I peer at the clouds. Gloomy and gray, they're blowing in fast, reflecting my mood. I feel like I'm driving on auto-pilot.

Once the farm is in another's hands, that's it. I won't be able to change my mind.

The rain picks up, and I turn my wipers on, searching for the local radio station to check the weather.

"This is Mikey Jay here, giving you the latest. If you're headed for Honey Falls, there's a car crash on Route 109 causing a ten-minute delay. Storm clouds are rolling in fast from the northwest. Rain and wind is expected through the afternoon and late into the evening. Stay safe, folks!"

I reach Bread & Bean as another gust rushes down the street. Finding a parking spot on Main Street, I ready my umbrella. Jogging to the coffee shop, I duck inside. Miranda waves at me from a table. She stands when I reach her and gives me an awkward hug. "Some weather we're having, right?"

I shuffle into my seat, putting my umbrella away. "I didn't expect it to get so bad so quickly."

"Summer flicks off like a light switch in Elmstitch." She settles onto her seat and pours another creamer into her coffee. "If you want to order something, go for it because we could lose power. I can wait."

I glance at the counter and then back to the windswept bushes on the curb. "I'm good. I haven't had much of an appetite lately."

She waves me off. "Coffee has nothing to do with appetite."

"You're right." I laugh. "It doesn't, but I'm still good." I twist my fingers together, trying not to fidget too much. Part of me wants to come right out and be clean with her... Another part, the old Delilah, urges me to keep silent. "How are you?"

"I'm good. I'm getting my supply ready for the fall season. I'm setting up a booth at Waverly's Pumpkin Patch next weekend. I always sell a lot this time of year."

"That sounds fun."

"It's great to see all the kids get their pumpkins."

"I bet."

Conversation fades as my attention is drawn to the front window where hail starts to clink against the glass.

I hope Hollowstalk's not working outside.

"Are you excited?"

I look back at Miranda. "What?"

"About going home? Are you excited?"

"Oh. Yes. I'm looking forward to it."

She takes a sip of her coffee. "You don't seem excited."

I thread my fingers together. "I have a lot on my mind."

"Are you okay?"

No. No, I'm not okay. I might be making the biggest mistake of my life. "Yeah, I'll be fine. We're harvesting this week. That's all."

"Oh, how fun!"

"Yeah."

I fall silent again, my gaze sliding back to the windows. "Miranda," I start, glancing back at her but hesitating, dropping my eyes to my wringing hands.

"You're having second thoughts, aren't you?"

Inhaling, I look up. She gives me a wistful expression that turns into a soft smile.

"I... am." It hurts even imagining saying goodbye. To Hollowstalk, the farm, the town, and even the crows. I never thought I'd grow attached to this place.

I can't imagine waking up without the farm that has stolen my heart. I'll miss coffee and morning jazz. Hollowstalk's uncanny grin.

I'll miss the forest and the crows, the long days of heat, and the heavy storms. The sound of caws in the wind. Fresh fruit and vegetables from the garden. I'll even miss Redeyes.

Hollowstalk's touch. The twinkle in his eyes. The way his fingers make me shiver whenever he touches me.

"It's okay to have second thoughts. If you need more time—"

In the distance, a siren goes off, cutting her off. A collective hush falls across the shop as conversations stall and heads rise. The barista, in the middle of making someone's drink, turns down the music.

"Tornado warning," someone says.

The windows shake as the wind gusts. The people sitting by them shift back. Some slip on their jackets and dart outside to watch.

Miranda pulls out her phone and stands. "Oh, dear."

My palms grow clammy as the lights flicker. "What's going on? Is there really a tornado? Should I be worried?"

"Can anyone see anything?"

One of the onlookers returns. "Yeah, I think there's a wall cloud, but I don't see a funnel."

Miranda faces me. "I should go."

The barista shouts, "Everyone, please head to the back!"

A wave of barely-suppressed panic falls across the remaining customers as they grab their things and retreat to the kitchen while several more leave.

Miranda heads for the door, and I chase after her, trying not to be swept up in the panic. "The sirens only go off if a tornado has been spotted."

My face turns ashen. "Should you go out there?"

She pauses and looks at me. "My son is visiting and is home with my dogs. He won't know how to help them. But I wouldn't go outside if I were you. I know what to look out for." She gives me a quick hug. "It was nice to see you, Delilah. We'll have to meet up another time. Stay safe and let me know what you decide."

She releases me and dashes out the door before I can say goodbye. Rain and wind blast my face the second it takes the door to swing shut.

Someone grabs my arm. "You should head to the back."

Seeing the barista, I tug out of her grip and rush outside. I need to get back to Crow's Rest and Hollowstalk.

If it gets dangerous, he'll come looking for me.

I shield my head with my arms, forgetting my umbrella as hail pelts the street. I pass another patron fleeing for their car as I head for mine. Nearly everyone has stayed in the coffee shop, and the realization makes my throat tighten. Whipping my hair and clothes back, the wind pushes against me. In a matter of minutes, it's gone from a simple thunderstorm to a nightmare.

Getting in my truck, I fumble with the keys. The sirens abruptly turn off.

I jump, wait a moment, then inhale sharply.

It's off. That's a good thing, right?

I start the truck and drive down the road. The few cars on the street are slow, maneuvering through the deluge at a snail's pace. With my vision obstructed by water, I clench the steering wheel, watching the road and searching the sky at the same time. At the next light, I turn on the radio.

"A tornado was seen making landfall past Elmstitch Square. So far no casualties have been reported and the funnel cloud has retracted. Stay inside, folks. Mikey Jay here, bringing you the latest."

Relieved, I wait for the stoplight to switch to green and cautiously accelerate. The rest of my chores will have to wait. More than anything, I want to be home and certain that Hollowstalk is fine. I don't want him to leave the grounds searching for me.

Because he would.

Driving past the farms and forests, I slow down at my turn. The truck bops switching from pavement to muddy road.

A dark form appears, and squinting at it, I realize it's a downed tree.

No.

I curse, pulling up to it and parking. Getting out, I search for a way around.

The clouds have an eerie green shade. My lungs fill with the scents of grass and dirt. Everything puts me on edge. I need to move.

There's no way around the tree. I climb back into the truck and curse some more, peering at the road behind me, unsure what to do. I force myself to calm down, listening to the rain, the wind, and the thunder.

I'm a little past the festival grounds. *I can do this.*

I grab my purse, and before I can reconsider, I step out, bow my head, and dodge around the tree. The wind rails against me as I stumble through several bushes. My shoes sink into mud as I stumble back to the road.

The sirens sound again, and at first, I'm not certain if I'm hearing them or if it's a ringing in my ears.

I try not to panic when Redeyes appears in the sky above. He caws as he circles over my head.

"Tell Hollowstalk I'm on my way!" I yell.

He caws and continues to circle.

"Go!" I shout.

When he flies away, I jog after him.

The trees thrash. Lightning flashes and my heart thunders as I leave the truck behind and close the distance between me and the farm, thinking about my next hot bath.

The road gets even muddier, and it gets harder to lift my feet, the winds slashing water at me from every direction as I slip on hail. The sirens go silent, and I see the first of Crow's Rest's cornstalks waving at me, swaying back and forth.

Exhaling with relief, I slow my pace.

"Delilah!" Hollowstalk shouts, my name barely audible above the wind when he sees me. He sprints down the driveway and hauls me into his arms when he reaches me. "Are you okay?"

Grabbing him back, relieved, I nod. He throws his trench coat around me, and we run toward the house as lightning flashes in the sky above.

Chapter Thirty-Six

THE CELLAR DEPTHS

Hollowstalk

I slam the door closed behind us. "We need to get to the cellar." I grab her arm again, glancing out the back window as I lead her toward the basement. Rain obscures my view, and the dark gray sky has turned day into night.

Delilah stops by the kitchen as I yank the cellar door open. She grabs a flashlight and, switching it on, rushes past me down the stairs. Dark shadows fill the window as I shut the door. The whole house shudders in a cacophony of creaking noises as the wind hounds the walls.

"Hollowstalk, come on!"

I jump the last steps and join her. At the back wall, we shuffle into the corner. I pull her under my arm. She's trembling, but the steadiness of her breaths consoles me, and I burrow my face into the top of her head.

I'd been pacing the driveway since the first sirens, afraid she might be in danger. The darkening sky, the sirens, I've experienced them before. Delilah is not familiar with what these ominous signs mean.

If Redeyes hadn't warned me she was down the road, I don't know what I would have done.

A vacuous hum fills my ears, soon joined by a screeching wind. Delilah jumps with each piercing shriek, and I rub her back, holding her tightly.

She jerks at the next boom.

There are several more before the house goes silent. Thunder roars from further away, and with each passing second, it grows fainter.

She pulls away when it fades altogether. "I'm soaking wet."

She's muddy and drenched from her trip to the farm, and I'm not much better.

I get to my feet. "Stay here. I'll go get us some towels."

"You don't think it's safe to go back up now? It's cold down here."

"Until the storm has passed entirely, we should remain below. The winds can pick up again. And fast. It's safest that way." I head upstairs to gather supplies and pause at the nearest window, inspecting the bruised clouds above and finding them not as dark as before. Lightning flashes, and I straighten away, remembering all the times I'd gone through storms exposed.

I grab a change of clothes and the crow skull necklace before returning to the cellar.

When I come upon her, she's staring at the empty shelves lining the back wall. Setting down some blankets and pillows, I join her with a towel and fresh clothes.

She points. "Does this wall look different to you?"

"You're shivering."

She doesn't protest as I turn her toward me and strip off her wet clothes.

"How is it up there?"

"It's fine for now, calmer than before." My greedy eyes rove over her wet, tight nipples and her farmer's tan. Gooseflesh prickles her skin, and I wrap her in the towel, covering her from my view, and dry her off.

She examines the clothes and narrows her gaze at me. "Really, Hollowstalk? No underwear?"

"You know I don't see the point of it."

She sighs and shuffles off my coat and pulls the sweatpants and T-shirt on. "Thank you for grabbing these at least." She dons the crow skull necklace last. My smile drops as I rush up the steps to shut the door. A powerful gust rattles the windows, and the sound follows me down the stairs.

I join Delilah next to the shelves, and she lifts her eyes as I approach. "Don't go back up."

"I won't."

"While we're waiting, look at this." She faces the wall again, shining the flashlight over it. "There's an indentation behind here."

She grabs the bulky wood shelves, inching them away from the wall. I nudge her aside and drag it the rest of the way until the entire wall is clear. I move back so she can run her light over it.

She points at a straight line in the brickwork. "I should've noticed this." Delilah frowns, trailing the light along the edges. "It's obvious without the shelves in front."

"Keep the light on it."

Moving forward, I run my hands over the lines, brushing the dust that has collected within their crevices. When I discover a small hole where a doorknob should be, I feel around for a latch. "There's something here."

I pull back on the latch, and it clicks up. The whole panel shifts, and when I push inward, the door scrapes across the floor. A cold, damp musk clouds me, and I shift to the side so she can shine her flashlight through, illuminating the hallway beyond.

It's short, the walls the same as the rest of the cellar, and on the other end is a closed wooden door. Between us and it, the walls are clustered with hanging herbs and half-melted candles atop shallow shelves. The damp, musky smell fades, quickly replaced by old plants with a hint of spice.

A hint of spice and weak magic.

Delilah walks down the hallway. "I feel like—" she shakes her head "—like I've been looking for this since the moment I got here. Is that strange?"

She glances at me.

I smile tightly, resting the heavy door in a wide position. Thunder rumbles above. "No. But we should be careful. It might not be safe."

"True."

At the other end of the small passage, we open the door together.

Inside is a midsize room much like the first part of the cellar. Unlike the front, it's filled to the brim with baubles and books. They're piled on rickety old tables and bookcases. There's an old desk to the left with a journal on top.

My flesh tingles, and I lean against the doorframe, sensing Winifred and every previous queen I have ever served within. A flash of the past two hundred years replays through my head.

I scowl at how much I have been denied, angry that Winifred trapped me in a body I couldn't move for so long.

My chest throbs with resentment.

It's a sensation I don't enjoy.

I peer at Delilah, who's perusing the bookshelf. She's talking, but the words are drowned out by the static crackling in my mind. Rubbing my chest, feeling my heart thrum beneath my skin, there's an ache there that wasn't there before.

"I love you," I say.

Delilah looks over her shoulder. "What?"

"I love you," I tell her again, pushing from the wall and closing the distance. "If you decide to go, I won't stop you. I will never take your freedom from you. I will never deny you. I need you to know that."

Her eyes soften as her brow wrinkles. "Hollowstalk... I... You love me?"

"So much it hurts." I caress her cheek.

Tears catch on her lashes, and I wipe them off with my thumb.

"I don't want to leave," she whispers so low I barely hear it. "I'm not ready. I don't want to say goodbye to you."

My fingers strain, clutching her harder, not sure if I heard her correctly.

"Then stay." I breathe.

"I'm scared."

I press my mouth to her brow. "Don't be, not with this."

"I can't help it. I'm so afraid you'll..."

"Turn back into a scarecrow?" I finish for her.

"Yes."

Wrapping my arms around her, I would sew us together, if I could. I would thread her body upon mine so we're never apart. "If I am only allowed to have one summer, then I am glad it was this one."

Her hands grip my jacket. "Please don't say stuff like that."

"Why not? I'm a romantic."

"Because it makes me feel like you're already trying to say goodbye to me."

"I'm right here," I tease, interrupting her. "I will never say goodbye to you. I've never said goodbye to anyone. I wouldn't start now."

That gets me a fleeting smile and a small laugh. She burrows her face into me. "I love you too, Hollowstalk."

I grin until my threads stretch. "I know."

"I needed that."

"I knew that too."

She grabs my collar and pulls me down, kissing the grin off my face.

I run my nose over the side of her face, breathing her in. "When we next fuck, please tell me you love me every time I thrust into you."

"I—" her face reddens "—okay. I will."

"Good, my queen." She doesn't know what her declaration of love has done to me, but I will make certain she does soon. I'm going to plant myself inside her and stay there. If I can't sew us together, I can still have this.

The creaking shrieks of the house intensifies, and I look down the hallway with a frown. There's a loud crash and a thrumming boom. Delilah freezes. Dust rains from the ceiling as the snapping sounds heighten. Neither of us move, we don't dare. With a ruckus, the door to the cellar slams back into place.

I draw her to the back of the room and move her under the desk. The shelves shake as the wind swoops into the space, blowing away papers and baubles. I crawl in after her and rest my chin on her head. "Don't be scared."

Thunder and lightning reign. The wind bellows, louder than before, and the house groans. There's an awful, tearing clatter. A riotous cacophony. And the sound of a slamming door.

Delilah stiffens.

"It'll be over soon," I assure her.

But my hands fall from her body.

The wind ebbs and fades, and she huddles further into me.

Pages flutter to the ground.

Limbs suddenly weakening, I rasp, "Delilah." I try to raise my arm but can't.

My voice is too weak to rise above the racket. My senses swirl as the dust settles, and the thunder grows distant... until it vanishes altogether.

No.

I swallow and choke. *Not now.*

Please.

Delilah, I try to say her name again, but my mouth won't move. My slowing heartbeat pounds in my ears.

Delilah.

She appears in front of me, her eyes wide and questioning. "Hollowstalk, what's wrong? Hollow—?"

She shakes me, but I don't feel it.

Her mouth opens and closes, saying things I can no longer hear. Things I would do anything to hear.

My body sags to the floor, and her tears fall on my cheeks. She rises over me, her glistening brown eyes filled with horror.

Don't be scared, I want to say.

But there's nothing I can do.

I smile at her instead, something to cheer her up, to let her know it will be okay, and then...

CHAPTER THIRTY-SEVEN

A DARK DAWN

DELILAH

Numbness comes and goes with my sobs.

Shuddering, I cuddle into Hollowstalk's limp form, clinging to him. No matter how many times I beg and curse, how many times I scream and shake him... He's gone.

He's gone.

A whisper of dawn light summons me back to my surroundings, commanding me to do *something*, anything. I can't stay down here forever, praying he'll wake up. The storm is over. It's a new day...

A cawing sound reaches me. *Redeyes.*

Startling, I peer about my surroundings in a new light, glancing over the shadowed shelves. I'd just begun to explore it last night, and now the contents are scattered about. My gaze drops back to Hollowstalk—his glass bead eyes, his sewn grin, and patched face.

Redeyes coos.

Blanking my mind against the pain, I lay Hollowstalk on his back. His arms bulge away from his sides, and his shoulders favor an angle as if he was propped against his pole. His hands are once again twigs.

His stitching is prominent, his skin deeply textured. He's composed of the same layers I have memorized, only now his eyes are lifeless. His hair falls awkwardly, and straw pokes out of his neck.

"Can you hear me?" I caress his cheek. "I need to leave. I have to see what's happened to the farm. Maybe it'll explain... this..."

I stand, staring down at him until the numbness returns. Exhaling the pressure in my chest, I walk down the short hall and face the door back to the cellar, now slammed back into place. When I push it, the door squeaks an inch. Heaving my weight against it, I force it a fraction wider.

The door scrapes against the floor upon my second push, caught by something on the other side.

Throwing all of my weight against it, I finally push it wide enough for me to squeeze through. On the other side, there's a broken pipe lodged against it. It almost trapped me inside.

I could be buried alive right now.

Redeyes caws from where he's perched on the cellar stairs, the daylight haloing him brighter than it should. I lift a hand to shade my eyes, squinting toward the source of the light. The washer and dryer have toppled into the cellar, and walking around them, I head toward the stairs and slowly climb them.

I promised him I'd be careful.

Ahead of me, where the den should be, the wall is missing. A breeze rustles my clothes as water drips on my shoulder. Climbing closer, I peer outside. The garden is gone, and the shed is nowhere in sight.

And the fields...

There isn't a single stalk of corn. Everything has been destroyed. Hollowstalk's platform is gone.

Redeyes flies to my side. Slowly, I give him a few short pats. Exhaling, I walk through the house to see what's left. I pass the kitchen and upturned dining room. The stairs to the second floor remain, but the living room is gone, taking my bedroom with it.

Outside, the old barn and the windmill are the only structures that remain intact.

Dazed and scared, I return to Hollowstalk. At the sight of him silent and still, I begin to sway. I pull his bulk into my arms anyway. Wrapping my arms under his and shuffling backward, I drag him out of the vault.

At the stairs, I take a moment's rest as Redeyes watches curiously from above. When he sees Hollowstalk, his feathers ruffle and he caws softly.

It hurts my heart.

It also makes me want to scream.

Lurching forward, I haul Hollowstalk up the stairs, through the ruins of the house, and into the windmill. Once inside, I prop him against the pole he made for me. "You'll be safe here."

With one last glance, I return to the front. The windmill, the barn, and the crooked house are all that remain. Tears stream down my cheeks.

Because I didn't just lose Hollowstalk.

I lost my home.

The crops.

And now...

I have to face the Crow King alone.

Chapter Thirty-Eight

THE QUEEN'S VAULT

DELILAH

Days pass, and Hollowstalk doesn't wake.

Spotting an ear of corn, I bend over and pick it up. After I check it over for damage, I drop it into my backpack and search for more.

Despite the cool, crisp morning, I wander through the empty fields as I've done every day since the tornado. Field and river, house and yard, I finally know every acre of old Crow's Rest, searching for anything blown away by the wind that is worth salvaging.

I'm on the lookout for Winifred's journal and the second crow skull.

Most importantly, I'm hunting for corn.

I've collected ten bushels so far, nowhere near enough to feed the crows through the winter. And it's all going to rot if I don't do something soon.

Where the fields meet the brook I pause, gazing at the water. Everything before almost seems like a dream now. Turning away, I pass through the forest which is now littered with broken branches and uprooted trees.

The house is gone. Everything is gone.

Even the magic is gone.

Redeyes caws for me. He's all that's left. He flies toward the windmill, and I follow after him.

Once home, I unzip my backpack and add the corn to my collection. Selecting one, I place it within the circle I've designed around Hollowstalk still propped on my pole. He's protected the corn for centuries, and I hope it can return the favor.

I wish I could ask him for advice or even just know if he can hear me, if he's aware. Every day he doesn't wake and nothing I try works, my depression worsens, my heart aches harder, and with them my dread grows.

Every day is one day closer to the deadline. The corn will soon rot. Should I offer what I have now?

The question haunts me as I leave the windmill and enter the barn to check the generator that luckily made it through the storm, along with the barn's running water. The last few nights, I've slept in the windmill. It's not much, but it's enough. I'd rather be out here alone anyway.

Redeyes stirs from his roost, sweeping out of the ajar barn door and toward the sound, and I'm following him outside when I hear the telltale sounds of a car pulling into the driveway.

Miranda parks out front, and sitting in the passenger's seat is Hopkins.

My throat tightens. I'm not ready for company. My emotions are raw and ripe.

She gets out of the car and rushes to me. "It's wonderful to see you're okay." She spreads her arms wide, and I find myself stepping into them.

I burst into tears.

She pets my back. "Oh, Delilah. I'm so sorry. I should have checked on you sooner. I knew you sounded off on the phone."

My first instinct is to pull away, but she doesn't let go, and so I continue to cry.

"When I heard the tornado landed near the festival grounds, I was so frightened." She gently releases me. "I saw you leaving the coffee shop. What the hell were you thinking?"

I was thinking about Hollowstalk. "I needed to get home."

She shakes her head. "I'm so glad you're safe."

I dry my eyes on my sleeve. "I'm sorry about the farm—"

"Honey, forget the farm." She pulls me into another brief hug. So much has gone wrong, but for the moment, she's right—*forget about the farm.*

When I pull away, my gaze catches on the emerald of Hopkins' cane, and he bows his head in acknowledgment.

"Hi," I say.

Miranda steps aside to allow him closer. "I mentioned wanting to check in on you, and he told me he knew you and asked to come along."

Hopkins shuffles nearer. "I hope that's okay with you."

"It's fine."

"Good." Miranda heads back to the car and pulls out clothes, soap, and a blanket. There's a bag full of energy bars, nuts, and another with bright red strawberries. "We brought some supplies."

I take the bags from her. "You're like the fairy godmother I didn't know I needed."

"Well, I don't know about that. If you need a place to stay—"

"I'm fine. I have electricity, water, and shelter."

"Delilah—"

"I really am fine. Honestly, it's easier for me to stay here. I have... a lot to clean up."

Hopkins taps Miranda with his cane. "I suspect Miss Mackey is as stubborn as Sylvie was."

She lifts a hand in defeat.

I thank him with a smile.

In return, he hands me a book I didn't see him holding before. "I've brought something for you too."

Taking the worn journal from him, I flip through the pages curiously, recognizing my aunt's handwriting. There are recipes, like a cookbook.

"I was borrowing it when she passed, and apologies, I forgot to give it to you. With the harvest coming up... I remembered I still had it. Sylvie always had plenty of food to share."

I smile, feeling a little better for the first time in a week. They carry on the conversation with little input from me, and I'm relieved to learn everyone is all right.

As the conversation winds down, Miranda laughs at something Hopkins says and gives me another hug. "Now don't be a stranger, okay? If you change your mind, I have a spare guest room."

"Thank you. I won't."

"You have my number," Hopkins reminds me.

"I do."

I watch as they get into the car and depart.

Afterward, I spend the rest of the afternoon reading the journal.

It's mostly a catalog of my aunt's recipes, with scribbled stories in between. Her first year she used roasted corn in a salad, writing that, *"Ivar loves it,"* with a heart drawn around it. Other recipes are marked *"for fertility."* At the end, it's empty pages, and I thumb through them, reaching the back of the book.

The last page is missing, torn from the spine. On the back of the previous page is a partial line.

...the present era. After failing to conceive, she secured an heir in town and was devastated when they died in a car crash. Upon divination, she names her niece as heir while still seeking out a way to contact her.

I stare at the blue lines until I'm sure—the timeline I found was torn from this journal. She must have ripped out the page with most of the information but forgot these final lines.

Still seeking out a way to contact her. What did that mean? If she had made any attempts, they never reached me.

And divination? My spine tingles, my body freezing like it did when I first saw my name in Winifred's journal. It was written in Winifred's hand, I'm sure of it, but when did it get there if Sylvie never saw it when she signed the book?

Magic must be involved. Somehow. As if from beyond the grave, Winifred wrote my name after I inherited the farm.

And if that's possible, there *has* to be a way to help Hollowstalk.

I flip back to the beginning and page through the entire thing again, searching for more, and it all clicks together when I find *"found in the vault"* written in the corner of one of the recipes.

Later at the house, I debate my way back in. I haven't gone into the cellar, let alone the vault, since I pulled out Hollowstalk.

I creep up the deck and pass through the dining room and kitchen. Turning on my flashlight, I descend into the cellar, and finally, the vault.

I gather the scattered papers and spread them out on the desk. They're damp, and the ink is blurry, making them impossible to read. Frowning, I turn to the cluttered shelves. Most of the books are journals. The rest of the shelves are filled with miscellany—crystals, poppets, and candles. The answers I'm looking for have to be somewhere in these.

For the next several hours I skim through everything until I find what I'm looking for...

A red box with a stack of thick papers and a short note on top.

For the preservation of Crow's Rest. —Mary Comings

It's documentation for an account at Elmstitch Bank.

And with it, Mary's depiction of her appeal to the Crow King.

CHAPTER THIRTY-NINE

A CROOKED HOME

DELILAH

After collecting years of accrued interest, Mary's old bank account, combined with my insurance claims, gives me enough money to rebuild the house and farm.

Winter is near, so I've opted for a patch job. What remains of the first floor has been salvageable by adding a wall to the remaining half of the house. The resulting space is small but functional.

I need it to stay through the winter and feed the crows. I dried out what limited corn I had and just ordered more. It might not all be blessed, but it's something to appease the Crow King.

And I *need* him appeased.

Hollowstalk still won't rise.

I've tried everything I can think of, creating rituals inspired by the contents of the vault. I've cleaned him, mended him, and found him new clothes. I've played him jazz and lit candles.

Nothing works.

All my hope now rides on next week, Halloween, when the harvest is due and spirits roam free.

It would be so easy to feel hopeless, and I'm glad Daniel is here.

My brother and I sit on a couch in the dining-turned-living room drinking a celebratory beer. Journey plays as we admire the newly built wall that now butts against the enclosed staircase.

He's leaving tomorrow.

Daniel sets down his beer. "I can't believe you're staying."

"I like it here."

"I know you do, but Mom thinks this is all her fault and she's failed you. That you're stuck here now, and she should have done more to prevent it."

I shrug. "I'll call her later."

He glances away, chewing over his next words. "She was raving about some weird stuff last night."

"Oh?"

"This is going to sound a bit extreme. And for the record, I think she had one too many cocktails... But she knew Sylvie was planning to give you the farm a couple of months before she died."

I frown. "She did?"

"Sylvie asked Mom for a way to reach you. She said it was important, going on about how special her corn was. Something about a crow—" he side-eyes Redeyes at his perch on the bookshelf— "and Mom told her you were working abroad and it would have to wait."

My stomach pits. "You're kidding, right? I never worked abroad."

"She said she did it to protect you."

I stare at him, stunned.

He flinches at me when he notices. "I'm sorry. I told her—"

Closing my eyes, I try to temper my anger.

"Doing okay?"

"Not exactly."

Daniel eyes me as he takes another drink from his beer. "Do some squats. They always calm me down."

"Squats?"

"Don't diss it until you try it."

It's annoying, but I stand up and do what he says out of spite. My breathing calms.

Damn it. He's right.

Daniel laughs. "See? A firmer butt solves all sorts of shit."

I throw a pillow at him, and he throws it back.

"I don't want to justify what she did, but I've been here long enough to know maybe Mom is on to something. I mean, for fuck's sake, Delilah, you have a giant red-eyed crow as a pet." He points at Redeyes who's grooming his feathers. "Mom's not just worried about nothing, is she?"

He doesn't even know that I'm wearing a crow skull necklace under my sweater.

I shake my head in answer.

He gazes warily at my crow. "I'm not asking you to tell me, but you need to know that I've got your back."

"I'm fine."

"I know that. You're a badass. And I'm sorry if I've never said that before."

I cross my arms and sit down beside him. "That's not what I expected to hear."

He shrugs. "I'm just saying whatever skeletons you're hiding in the windmill, I know you'll handle them. But I'm here, and these muscles aren't only to impress the girls." He bunches his bicep.

I lean against his arm and smile. "Thanks. That means a lot coming from you."

He pulls me close. "So... now that that's out of the way, can I see what's inside the windmill?"

I laugh. "No."

He's opening his mouth for a rebuttal when his phone dings. Pulling it out of his pocket, he looks at the screen and grins.

Sitting back, I try to peek at his screen. "It's Caitlin, isn't it?"

"Oh, shut up." He taps away at his phone. "I've told her about the steroids. And it's going to be a problem—she wants to have kids, and with the drugs, I'm not sure if I can. The relationship is not gonna go anywhere."

I eye him. "Why not? You could stop."

He lifts his eyes. "I'm thinking about it."

"Wow. That's... huge."

"I know, I know, easier said than done. But one of my old buddies quit a few years ago, and we've reconnected. He's given me some tips."

I punch his shoulder. "I've got your back too."

"Thanks." He puts his phone away. "So what happened to that guy who was here last time?"

Leaning back onto the couch, I polish off my beer. "Jack's on a trip, but he'll be back soon."

Chapter Forty

HOLLOW'S EVE

Delilah

The night before Halloween, I shower and dress, taking the time to organize my hair in a tight, tidy braid. The Crow King has a taste for pageantry, and I don't want to screw anything up. For a final touch, I don the crow-skull necklace.

Pleased with my appearance, I scatter the perimeter of the windmill with dried corn and place the last of it at Hollowstalk's feet.

I'm not certain when the Crow King will appear, assuming he appears at all. Mary's records say her parents were turned to crows at dawn, but I'm planning on staying up all night and have come prepared with a gigantic thermos of coffee.

Pacing in circles, I try not to look at Hollowstalk for too long as the hours bleed into one another.

Dawn comes and goes, and I'm about to give up and try a different approach when I hear a caw outside.

Daylight streams through the door's cracks, catching on motes of dust. It's strange, brighter than it should be. Cold pierces my bones as I head to the door, my limbs fluid, like I'm floating through the air.

A dark shadow appears on the other side, blocking out the light. Inhaling, I debate whether or not to let him in.

They knock.

"The Crow King?"

"Indeed."

His deep voice shakes me. My nerves fire, and I quell the urge to panic.

It's now or never.

I'm going to face a god. A forest god. A primitive supernatural being I didn't even know existed several months ago. I wish I didn't know how I got here, but I do. I glance at Hollowstalk for courage, praying for every ounce I can muster.

Opening the door, I step outside. Squinting against the brightness, I blink until I can see.

The Crow King is neither a figure nor a shadow. He's a crow so large he could be ridden. His long pitch black feathers are sleek and pointed at the end of his tail like thin blades.

Awed, I straighten, finding him not as frightening as I thought he would be. "Yes. We should talk. What happened to Hollowstalk?"

Unmoving and intimidating, he opens his beak wide. "That lifeless doll you're still holding on to?"

"He's not—"

"What remained of Winifred's power has left him. And what remains is now... about."

My gaze drifts past his wing, finding there are crops here, lush and green—their color is a little too vivid and straight out of a dream. "What do you mean, he's *about*?"

He abruptly shrinks and takes on the form of a man, and I take a step away as he comes to stand before me. He blinks with entirely black eyes. His high-waisted pants leave his chest exposed, showing his velvety gray skin. His black hair is streaked with feathers that cascade down his back to pool around his bare clawed feet.

He considers me, but without pupils, I can't tell where he's looking. Light catches in his eyes as if they were glassy mirrors. But when I try to look at myself in them, all I see are stars.

I take another step back.

"I am so very... curious," he says.

I tear my gaze away. "Curious?"

"You brought Hollowstalk to life, didn't you? Even if it was by accident. The last of Winifred's magic had remained both in Hollowstalk and in the house, living on long after her death. With her artifacts lost to the storm, what bound Hollowstalk to the living was also destroyed. Your scarecrow is gone because there was nothing left to keep him here."

My lips part. "He needs to be attached... to something?"

The Crow King hums without answering me. "He sewed on a cock for you. At first his decision surprised me, but maybe I'm starting to see the appeal."

Pretending to be confused by what he means, I shake my head. "I'm here to discuss the terms of the pact."

"Of course. You have failed your end." He sweeps away. "We should discuss that first." He points a taloned finger at me that slowly curls inward.

I eye him warily. "The crows won't go hungry. I've secured enough food for them through winter."

"It's a good gesture. Except the principle remains. The land is blessed with prosperity, and that prosperity is meant to be fed to my crows."

"That may be so, but there have been outlying circumstances as I'm sure you're aware of, and since you need your crows to be fed and your blessing failed to keep the tornado away, you need me. So I've prepared my terms."

"It is so unfortunate that only humans have hands." He sighs, gesturing at me. "You came to this farm intent upon abdicating. Why change your mind? Is it perhaps the scarecrow?"

I see no reason to lie to him. "Yes. It's because of Hollowstalk."

"Interesting."

My brow scrunches. "Why is that interesting?"

"You're a human and he's..." The Crow King flicks his finger again like he's searching for a word.

"Not?" I offer him.

"Yes. *Not*. He's *not* anything."

I press my tongue to the roof of my mouth, hating the pain his words cause me. Because Hollowstalk is *everything* to me. The very fact that the Crow King calls him nothing makes Hollowstalk mean all that much more. "I want to change the pact's terms."

"And why would I allow that?"

"Because I'm willing to offer something better, something more."

"Better than food?" He laughs. "Is there such a thing?"

"The fact that you can joke at a time like this lowers my opinion of you significantly." My eyes narrow.

He opens his mouth and... caws at me.

Frowning, I cross my arms over my chest and look away uneasily. "Return Hollowstalk to life and bind him to me. In exchange, I'll remain at Crow's Rest and care for the crows, not only during the winter but the entire year, and will continue to do so for the rest of my life." I watch his face.

He taps his lips. "I have another offer. Would you like to hear it?"

"What is it?"

"Ensure the crows are fed through the following winter, and then we are done. Your debt would be forgiven and the pact dissolved."

I study him, searching for his trick. That sounds too good to be true. "I didn't realize something like that would be an option."

His eyes twinkle. "This agreement is old, and I have come to wonder if perhaps the pact has overstayed."

"What would happen to Hollowstalk?"

"He'll remain as he is now and not the vile miscreant who frightens my flock and slashes their beautiful feathers with his scythe."

"Hollowstalk is non-negotiable."

He turns toward the house. "Is he? Then I will offer you a third option." He takes a few steps away, and after a moment's hesitation, I follow.

The crops spread into a path before him. "You could find him."

I look down the path into the field. More rows open up, presenting me with countless options. "In a maze?" I frown.

"If you find him, I'll return him to what he was upon his death and bind him to you. In exchange for my generosity, you'll remain here for the rest of your life and not only feed my flock year-round, but you will no longer frighten them—you must celebrate them. You and the scarecrow will be blessed with the fertility to reproduce and ensure your lineage continues so this agreement might be honored for the next hundred years."

My fingers tremble, and my palms grow clammy. I glance beyond him and at the ocean of corn at his back because I believe he's telling the truth—Hollowstalk is somewhere in that maze, and the Crow King won't give him to me without sacrifice.

A hundred years. I know it from the way my heart throbs against the skull necklace that I'm going to accept. Especially if... it means we can have children together. Children I'll need to shield from being bound in the future. But if everything else is possible, I'll find a way to live so long it never matters.

Looking past him, the maze darkens as fog emerges. "What happens if I don't find him?"

The Crow King faces me, returning his unnatural gaze to me. "You'll become mine forever." He smiles. "The decision is yours to make, Delilah. Return to your old life or save Hollowstalk and remain here until your demise. Choose wisely."

Giving him my answer, I stride past him and into the stalks.

He caws, and the corn closes behind me.

CHAPTER FORTY-ONE

THE JOURNEY HOME

HOLLOWSTALK

Thump. Thump.

I listen harder, tracing the sound, hungry for more of it, driven by a need I can't justify. A woman with brown hair and piercing eyes.

I've felt this before, only then I was led by the beat of a drum and not a heart.

Winifred.

When I open my eyes, she's there with a drum on her lap. As I stare down from my post, she appears as she did when I was first formed.

"You're awake," she whispers.

I can't respond, can't move.

She stops beating on the drum, which doesn't seem right—because the rhythm doesn't stop with her. The thumping sounds louder.

"You've found yourself a heart. You don't need this anymore." She sets the drum to the side and squints up at me. Following her gaze, I notice that my leather body is stained and my burlap skin is frayed. "Your queen seeks you out."

My queen?

Delilah. The brown-haired woman. The one who tugs at my heart.

She is the reason I need to... *move.*

Winifred smiles at me and walks away.

Move.

"Hollowstalk!" My name rises from the distance, and I feel it again—*thump, thump.*

Delilah, I try to say her name, but my lips won't move.

My heartbeat quickens, but my limbs remain stiff.

"Hollowstalk!"

She yells for me, and I call out in return. Nothing leaves my throat.

"Hollowstalk!" she shouts again.

I tense, my mind caught by an onslaught of memories. A breeze sways the stalks around me, lulling me. I remember warmth. Golden mornings of coffee, dance, and jazz. The color of the sun catching in her hair.

"Hollowstalk!"

Delilah's voice is farther away.

My memories of her begin to fade.

Stiffening, panic seizes my threads. Fear. Terror. Every emotion I once enjoyed turns against me. *Move!*

Snapping out my arm, I reach behind me to grab my scythe.

"I'm here," I rasp, gripping it and pulling the rest of my bound limbs free.

There's no answer.

"Delilah!" I bellow at the top of my voice. At the sound, thousands of crows flee into the sky.

Somewhere throughout it all, I hear Delilah shout for me again.

Brandishing my weapon, I slash through the corn and toward it. "I'm here!" I cut down every single stalk between me and her, refusing to stop even when my limbs shake and my threads break. After what seems like an eternity, she appears when the last one falls, her lips parted, her chest heaving like she's been running nonstop.

"Hollowstalk," she breathes upon seeing me.

I lower my scythe. "My queen."

She cries out and runs into my arms. Holding her close, I bury my face in her hair.

"I found you," she mutters against my chest, pressing her face into it. "I finally found you."

"I'm here now. It's okay." But as I say this, I look around, recognizing nothing about the decimated field we're in. "Where are we?"

"The Crow King offered me a chance to bring you back," she says against my chest.

I frown and pull away to look at her. "Back?"

"You... faded, Hollowstalk. The storm destroyed Crow's Rest. Almost everything is gone."

The storm. New memories flash through me. *The storm...*

She's right. I faded. That means...

I grip Delilah's shoulder and meet her gaze. "You met with the Crow King? What day is it?"

"Halloween. It doesn't matter." She tries to reassure me when she sees my face harden. "The pact has been renegotiated. All I needed to do was find you... I'll care for the crows until I die.

We'll be able to have children. I'd love to tell you more about it, but right now…" Her lips drop. "We need to find a way out of here."

I freeze. "You agreed to stay?"

"Yes." She pauses.

I search her face. "For the rest of your life? Why?"

If she agreed to this, she's bound. Like me.

"I want to stay. I thought I lost you and… I couldn't go back," her voice lowers into a whisper. "I don't want to return to who I was, pretending this summer never happened. Everything I want is here, with you. I know that now." She lifts the crow skull necklace from her chest and, standing on her tiptoes, lowers it over my neck.

Finally, her love is mine. Cupping her face, my fingers shudder against her skin.

Tears form in her eyes as I stare at her.

"Hollowstalk." She reaches up and pulls me down into a kiss.

But our lips never touch.

Blinking, I look around. I'm leaning against the post inside the windmill with dried corn at my feet. Rising to my feet, I take hold of my scythe on the ground next to me.

The door opens, shining daylight on my face.

The Crow King appears, human in his appearance.

He doesn't say anything before he turns into the shadow of a crow and flies away.

Delilah appears in his wake, stopping short upon seeing me her ashen face floods with excitement.

Running forward, I catch her in my arms and run my fingers through her hair. Kissing her, I lock my scythe around her, a warning to all who would dare to come between us again.

CHAPTER FORTY-TWO

THE REVERENCE OF CROWS

DELILAH

Walking hand in hand, I give Hollowstalk a tour of the crooked house. There's so much to tell him about the last month.

I can't stop grinning. It's unreal that he's here.

I'm showing him the vault, now organized and clean. My stomach knots, remembering that the last time we were down here together, I lost him. Except the space is different now, changed by all the hours that I've spent studying since.

He steps closer, caging me against the desk. "You've done well. You impress me, Delilah."

Loving his praise and embarrassed by it, my cheeks warm. "I had to get you back."

"Your renegotiation..." he pauses. "You said we will have children now?"

"The continuation of my line was part of the deal." I can't read his expression, and my stomach pits. "I know we never talked about children. I hope it's okay—"

He lifts my chin so my gaze meets his. "I just never thought... never imagined..." He blinks. "Me, a father?" Then he growls. "I cannot wait to fill your belly with my seed."

Laughing, I push at his chest, surprised by how arousing his dirty words are, and I vow to fill the bookshelves with romances. "Now you're the one making me nervous."

"Nervous?"

"I'm not quite ready. I want to rebuild the house—have a proper nursery—and then there's the crows..."

"When can we start?"

"At least a year, maybe longer." I lift my chin and kiss him.

He deepens the kiss, and I'm wrapping my legs around his waist when we're interrupted by a ruckus of caws.

I lean back. "What in the world are they up to?"

The mayhem continues as we leave the vault and head outside.

The field is entirely covered by crows, and as the door opens, their cawing worsens. Covering my ears, I glance at Hollowstalk. They're noisy and rambunctious, flapping their wings in excitement.

Suddenly it goes quiet, and the birds are still, staring at me with their dark, beady eyes.

Redeyes flies from the forest, landing at the head of their ranks. When he cants his head, I see he's holding something in his beak.

Winifred's journal.

He hops forward, sets it down, and then takes a few steps back.

"I looked for this," I tell the bird. "Have you had it this whole time?"

He ruffles his feathers and caws toward Hollowstalk.

"The Crow King needs you to sign it," he says.

"Oh."

I go back inside the house to find my nicest pen, and by the time I return, Hollowstalk is reading the book, staring at the page with his manual.

I peer over his shoulder, giving him this curiosity. I've spent my summer paging through this document and know it all too well.

Except when he turns the page, I realize it's not like it was. The section called *The Pact* has new amendments, each of them written in Winifred's hand, and it looks like they describe everything the Crow King and I agreed to.

I reach for the book, and Hollowstalk hands it to me with a kiss to my brow.

Sitting down, I pore over it, checking for any hidden amendments. Mary's account of her negotiation never mentioned changes to the book—but she also didn't change the terms of the pact—though she did say she had to sign it.

Once I'm satisfied, I turn to the final page and stare down at the blank signature line next to my name.

And without another doubt, I sign, *Delilah Rose Mackey, the Seventh and Final Queen of Crow's Rest.*

EPILOGUE: CROW'S REST FAIRE

DELILAH

I scamper from the vendor stalls and into the house. Miranda is running low on napkins, and I have a spare pack inside. I weave my way through the visitors, noticing we seem to have more of them with each passing year.

Crow's Rest Sanctuary is that, most of the time, a *sanctuary*.

This weekend, that of October 14th, is the main exception. What started as a public relations project—a little music, some dancing, and of course food—is now an annual tradition.

The renovated house resembles the old one with a wrap-around porch, except the structure is bigger. We lost three-quarters of the place during the storm, and renovations took the better part of a year. The result is a four-bedroom house with a new room where the sunroom once was.

Some of the rooms are still empty and bare, but getting the nursery done is the highest priority.

Crow's Rest is unrecognizable from when the tornado hit three years ago.

On my way to the pantry, I pass by the living room where sitcom reruns play quietly on the TV. Daniel is here, and he brought his family—Caitlin and their six-month-old twins. They're each holding one of the babies as they doze on the couch, and at the sight, I press my hand to my own growing belly.

I'm five months pregnant, and the reality that I'll soon have a baby girl is kicking in. Daniel has been teasing me about sleepless nights.

Meanwhile, Mom picks at her nails.

It's her second visit. The first one was my wedding to Hollowstalk—or Jack Hollow, as everyone else knows him. It was a small, intimate affair in the backyard. I loved it while Mom hated it.

"Everything good here?" I ask.

Daniel gives me a thumbs up.

Mom shrugs and picks up a magazine from the coffee table. "Wonderful."

Napkins in hand, I return to Miranda.

"You didn't need to do that," she chastises me, tearing open the pack and placing a pile of napkins at the front of her booth. "You should be resting. I would have gotten to it eventually."

"It's fine. There are more guests than we expected. Next year we'll hire an extra set of hands."

"Good idea."

"And it's no bother. I feel better than I have in a while." I press a hand to my back, massaging the aches there.

Miranda scans me over then returns her attention to her grill. "Jack's worried about you."

I sigh. "I'm fine. He knows I hate being stationary. I keep telling him that."

Miranda smiles as she greets the next customer.

Stepping out, I take a deep breath and scan the yard.

Visitors mill about the small park where the scarecrow platform used to be. Beyond, there's a space for vendors and a stage. Plaques are posted throughout with facts and information about the crows.

The birds watch the onlookers with curiosity.

Hopkins walks up to me, the emerald of his cane flashing as he taps it against the ground.

I smile at him. "I'll be coming by the shop next week. I've found something of Sylvie's that might be of some interest to you." There is no need for pretense with him—I've since visited his hidden library, finding its contents similar to my vault.

He raises an eyebrow. "I look forward to it."

Nodding, I scan the crowd another time. "Have you seen my husband?"

"He's at the graveyard."

"Thanks."

I weave my way past the crowds, grabbing my bike as I take off into the fields beyond the sanctuary.

Above, Redeyes follows, circling the sky.

The fields are lush and growing well. Hollowstalk has never lost the gift for growth. We sell his crops locally or preserve them for the crows.

I approach the old ground, finding the graveyard tidy and the stones neat. Hollowstalk stands with his back to me, his patches showing. In this company, he doesn't pretend to be fully human.

Hopkins has... introduced us to others who are like us.

Like Summer and Zuriel.

Redeyes gets the attention of Summer's cat, and Ginny meows loudly, her tail twitching. The crow lands several feet away, straightening his neck. She licks her paw, and they settle into a familiar indifference.

Hollowstalk turns at my approach. Summer and Zuriel are at his side, and it looks like they are examining Winifred's stone—it's not the first time they've visited it during their studies on ghosts. They, like us, are exploring how to expand the human lifespan, and Hopkins has given their work a head start.

I pedal to them. "I thought you wouldn't be back for a few more days."

They've been gone for over a month, driving throughout the country. First they went north to the mountains and then west to the coast. They were acquiring things for the museum. I don't understand half of it, but Summer was pretty excited when Hopkins asked them to take the trip.

Summer's finger glistens as a small diamond catches the light.

She lifts her hand as I notice, beaming at me. "Yep, we're engaged! Long story short, I said yes." She glances at Zuriel.

Towering over her, even in his human form, Zuriel reminds me of a gargoyle. With his height and large build, he intimidates even Daniel—which is fun to watch.

She grabs my arm and starts leading me back toward the fair. "How have you been, is the pregnancy treating you okay?"

Getting off the bike, I wheel it as we walk side by side and fill her in on all the gruesome details, appreciating someone new to complain to.

She, Zuriel, and Hopkins, are some of the few who know I'm not having a normal go at it. I can't risk seeing an obstetrician. Instead, Hopkins introduced me to a special doctor, one who deals with... situations like this.

Later that day, once the guests are gone, we settle on the porch. Finally, it's just Hollowstalk and me. He puts on jazz, and I lean back with a sigh as he tugs off my shoes and starts massaging my foot. I surrender with a light moan.

"You push too hard," he scolds.

"I'm pregnant, not fragile. Anyway, it's good to stay active."

He switches to my other foot, and I relax into his touch, slumping deeper into my chair. I grumble when he wraps me in his arms and pulls me to his chest. "Why did you have to stop?" I whine.

"Because I've got a surprise for you."

"You do?" I murmur, hoping his surprise is an antacid that lasts forever because I've considered making another deal with a forest god for just that. "Is it watermelon and pickles?" I ask instead.

He laughs and to my fervent disappointment leads me to the stairs rather than to the kitchen. "Miranda is dropping some off tomorrow."

"It's not soon enough," I whine some more.

"I think I can help make the time pass so it doesn't hurt so much."

Eyes glistening with hope, I look at him. "Promise?"

Laughing some more, he leads me to the nursery and opens the door. "I promise. Surprise."

The walls have been painted, and the floorboards are now in place. Everywhere I look there are sunflowers and bumblebees, painted on the walls, pictured in frames, and as fluffy stuffed animals.

"I love it," I whisper.

He puts his hands on my shoulders. "For the flower we created."

Sniffling, I turn in his arms and hug him. "I love it. I love you. Sunflowers and bumblebees. It's perfect."

He combs my hair. "It was your mom's idea."

I blink back tears. "It was?" I sniffle.

"While everyone kept you distracted, she bought everything and decorated it. She insisted."

Facing the room, I step into the beautiful golden space and caress my fingers over the padded rocking chair and bumblebee mobile, taken back to when I was a kid and my mom decorated my room with flowers. "I'll have to call her in the morning."

He leads me from the nursery and into our bedroom. And while he runs a bath for me, I head to the window and look outside.

Twilight paints the field, turning everything a deep purple. The forest darkens in the distance, blending the trees into one large shadow in the shape of a crow. I shut the drapes.

Hollowstalk leads me into the bathroom where a tub of warm water waits for me.

Throwing out his hand, he grins and bows his head. *"My queen."*

He kneels as I shuffle out of my clothes, his eyes cast on the floor. Standing before him, I lift his chin. *"My king."*

His expression is deliciously wicked, marked by a grin that once frightened me. I lean against his chest and listen to its beat—finding its rhythm synced to mine as it always is these days—and smile. My scarecrow has found a heart.

AUTHORS' NOTE

THANK YOU FOR READING *The Scarecrow's Queen*! If you liked the story or have a comment, please leave a review or rating!

www.ingramcontent.com/pod-product-compliance
Lightning Source LLC
Chambersburg PA
CBHW051219130726
47988CB00001B/140